FATE'S BITE SERIES

HALF
TRUTHS
THEN

I'M HER RAGE. SHE'S MY GODDESS.

ELENA M. REYES

SUMMARY

I'M A BEAST.
UNTAMED.
WILD.

I have no need for a mate, much less a witch. Her kind is untrustworthy and cruel, yet this one beckons me, and the pull is near volatile. My wolf thirsts for her pinned beneath us while my teeth break flesh—mark her as ours.

Rejecting her is right, but at what cost?

It's the first time the animal and I are at odds. A KING does not bend the knee.

Yet this is a simmering thirst I've fought to keep locked away; it doesn't get to come out and play often, but I do enjoy the moments when I let go of the reins. Each time we meet, I crave more. Each time she gives me her back while walking away, the walls I've erected in her name break until what's left is wrapped around her slim finger.

I am her rage. She is my goddess.

Together they create what I am: a vengeful animal determined to protect what's mine.

HALF TRUTHS: THEN
(Fate's Bite #3)
was written by Elena M. Reyes
Copyright 2022 ©Elena M. Reyes

Cover Design: T.E. Black

Editor: Marti Lynch

Publication Date: October 28th 2022
Genre: FICTION/Dark Romance/Erotica Suspense/Thriller
Copyright © 2022 Elena M. Reyes
All rights reserved.

ACKNOWLEDGMENTS

This one's for those who believe in soul mates. Who love a brooding alpha, a man with an edge of violence, and who will burn the world to the ground for his woman.
These two books will test you, but trust me.
I'm a PNR whore who lives for a good HEA #HePurrs.

HAPPY READING, MY BEAUTIFUL BABES!!!

Also, a huge THANK YOU to my team. Seriously, I couldn't do this without you.

Ana Rita, C.M. Steele, Marti Lynch, Emina Ros & Tonya Fox Summerlin; I LOVE YOU WITH ALL MY HEART. I couldn't do this without your help, push, & love. How you threaten me when I need the kick. This book is finished because each of you.

And to my husband: You will always be my boyfriend. My muse.

XOXO

Elena

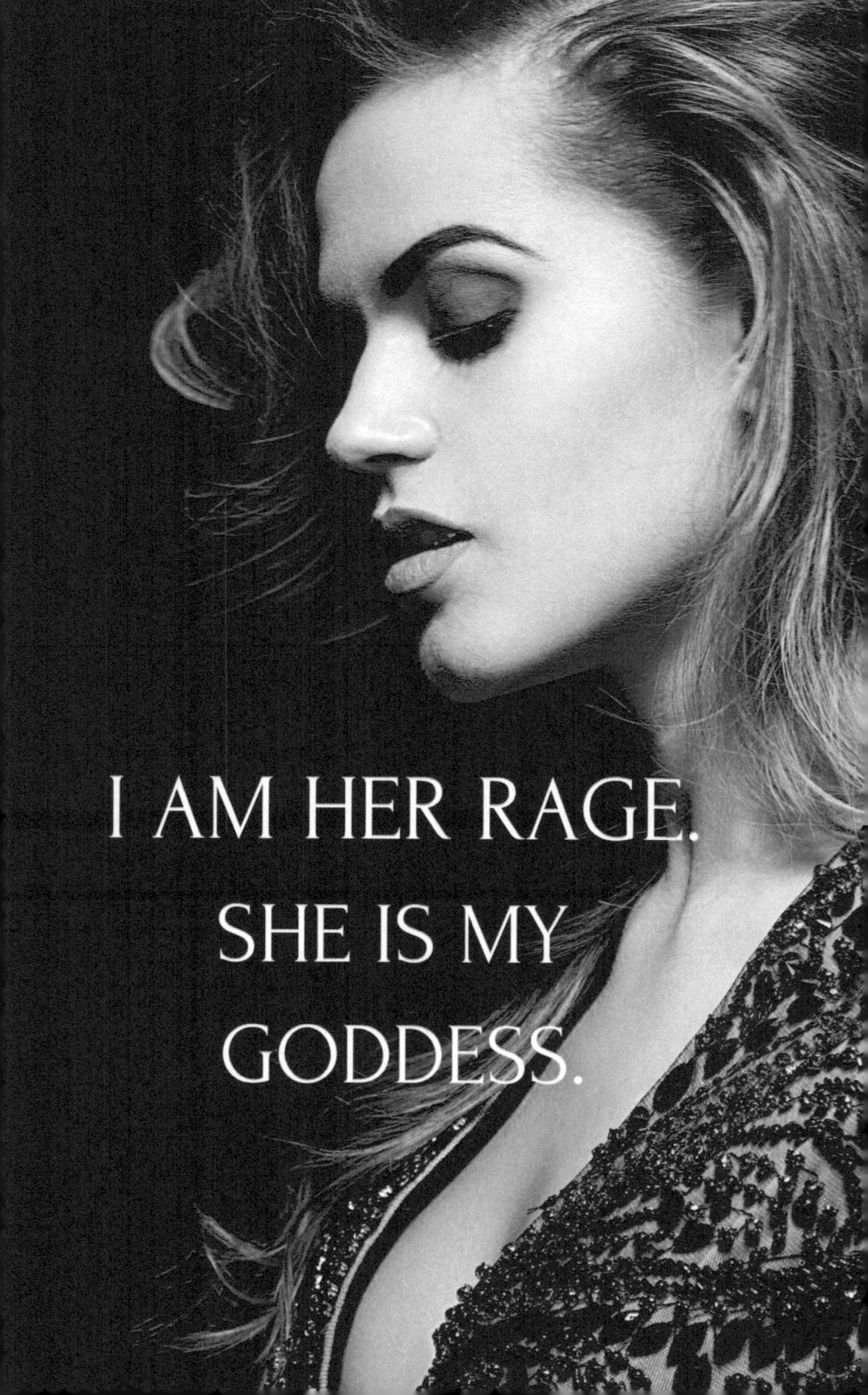

I AM HER RAGE.
SHE IS MY
GODDESS.

HALF TRUTHS THEN

Playlist

BECOME THE BEAST BY KARLIENE
THE HEART WANTS WHAT IT
WANTS BY SELENA GOMEZ
LOVE IS A BITCH BY TWO FEET
BLACKEST HAND BY SAINT MESA
SEVEN NATION ARMY BY FUTURE ROYALTY
PLAY WITH FIRE BY SAM TINNESZ
& YACHT MONEY
FROZEN BY MADONNA, SICKICK, & 070 SHAKE
INFINITY BY JAYMES YOUNG
WEREWOLF HEART BY DEAD MAN'S BONES
I WANT TO BY ROSENFELD
HORNS BY BRYCE FOX
ALL THE GOOD GIRLS GO TO HELL BY BILLIE EILISH
WICKED GAME BY URSINE VULPINE & ANNACA
NEVER TO LATE BY THREE DAYS GRACE

FATE'S BITE SERIES

HALF TRUTHS THEN

playlist

IT'S NOT OVER BY DAUGHTRY
ZOMBIE BY BAD WOLVES
WOULD THAT I BY HOZIER
CLOSER BY J2 & KEELEY BUMFORD
TOXIC BY NINA NESBITT
MURKY BY SAINT MESA
WOLF BY SAINT MESA
DIRTY THOUGHTS BY CHLOE ADAMS
SEX AND CANDY BY ALEXANDER JEAN
MIDDLE OF THE NIGHT BY ELLEY DUHE
CHERRY PIE BY WARRANT
MAN OR MONSTER BY
SAM TINESZ & ZAYVE WOLF

GLOSSARY

Mind link communications are in ***bold italic***.

Alpha King: Ruler of all werewolf packs. Also referred to as alpha of alphas

Luna: His Queen & Mate

Beta: Second-in-command, but under the Luna

Gamma: Third-in-command, also under the Luna

Pack: Community of werewolves; family

TRIGGER WARNINGS:

This book contains dark elements that some readers might find triggering. This man is brutal and unapologetic, please read at your own discretion.

Contains:

Explicit Violence
Death & Torture
Biting/Mating Mark
Some Primal Play
Obsessive Anti-Hero
Knotting

1
ALPHA
XADIEL

J asmines.

Sweet motherfucking jasmines.

The scent is soft in the wind, like a mystical calling, and I stop to take it in. The beast and I are entranced, need to find this blooming scent with a small note of white musk that's awakened my cock while out on a moonlit run.

My claws dig into the forest floor, muzzle high in the air as a hungry rumble builds in my chest.

I'm alone. The animal in me is in control, and yet I'm conscious of his every move.

We're two beings who share a body and soul. He is me, and I am him.

Ears back, I listen for movement. There's a lake close to where I am, but before I give in to the hunt, another scent mingles with my night bloom. I let out a low warning growl, a deep and angry rumble that lets the guards on duty know I'm here. They know better than to come near me on a run like this one. My wolf is different than others and prefers his solitude while hunting; he's been hungry for the fresh taste of wild game, but now another desire controls us.

My apologies, Alpha.

One of the guard's thoughts comes through the mind link before I sense them scurrying away, but I don't respond. Not when I take another step toward the sweet scent. When with each move forward my bones reshape. They crack and shift, forcing my black fur back as bones realign and my tanned skin prickles with goose bumps.

I vibrate with a deep sense of yearning; one I've never encountered before in my ninety years walking this earth. It slams into me while the cooling mist left from an earlier rain shower caresses my naked flesh. Chest expanding, I take in deep breaths while my muscles contract—my fangs drop—and a new kind of desire settles on the tip of my thick cock.

Another step, and I feel a few beads of pre-come slip from the engorged head and onto the forest floor, leaving behind a trail from my moment of weakness.

I'm throbbing. My limbs tremble.

At seven feet, I'm a beast in my human form too.

We're on the west side of my land and away from the pack that lives near the castle, and yet, I'm finding myself jealous of anyone scenting the owner of this seducing perfume. This heady note is making me forget both my duty and the one purpose in my life I'm yet to fulfill.

I have a warlock to find. A protected queen to kill.

Their combined blood dripping from my muzzle to savor.

And yet, I'm more concerned at the moment with keeping this precious scent to myself.

Mine. All motherfucking mine.

Without conscious thought, I grip my length and stroke, never pausing in my search. It leads me about half a mile deeper into the woods and toward the edge of a clearing. The beast is present in my eyes; I feel his sharp awareness mingling with my own and if my prey were to turn around, she'd find golden eyes watching her every move. My heightened senses give me the honor of taking in the most minute details, from her skin to her hair and then the small beauty mark at the center of her back.

And *motherfuck,* Little Red is ethereal. Her lithe form is facing away from me while walking slowly into the edge of a small lake surrounded by tall grass and wildflowers. Naked, and with the moon shining over her soft skin and highlighting the fiery shade of her tresses, she wades in deeper while emitting a soft sigh when the water comes up to the very tip of her round arse.

This woman is bloody perfection.

She's also made for me. There's no doubt about that.

My mate.

I've never searched for her but instead waited patiently. I've never touched another, never gave in to temptation because doing so would be a stain on us. On the bond we'd forge and nurture.

Instead, I trained and fought and protected my lands. A king is never in short supply of those willing to spread their legs, both women and men, trying to win favors for their house and name, but my people know better than to try with me. I'll always be faithful no matter the circumstance.

Moreover, I watch her with my fangs piercing my bottom lip and hips pumping against my hand without shame. Tightening my fist, I twist on the upstroke and then swipe my thumb across the slit, using the wetness there to fuck my hand.

I take in how she cups the water in her tiny hands and then brings them up, just high enough to flow down her neck and chest. Each rivulet glides over her bare flesh before disappearing beneath the calm waters, and I'm jealous of each drop. This happens a few more times, those fingers wiping across her chest and stomach before she arches back and stretches her arms high.

The breeze sweeps across us a little harder just as her head tips back, and that mouthwatering scent smacks into my senses with the force of a battering ram. My balls swell and I grind my teeth hard, fighting back the urge to come. *Not until I'm inside of her.* With that vow, I give myself another three punishing strokes and release my hold, hissing when the hard-as-steel flesh gives a violent jerk in the night air.

"My little moon," I groan out, stepping out from under the tree I'd taken a pause under, but then she dips underneath the water. For sixty agonizing seconds, she submerges herself, but before I can rush in after her, she breaks through the surface, eyes closed and facing me.

Once again, the lake laps against her arse, gently swaying against her skin.

Every cell in my werewolf DNA expands and demands I accept her.

My beast vows to protect and cherish her.

I take in this beautiful woman from my position at the shore, memorizing every dip and sinuous curve, from the wide set of her hips and flat stomach to the perky set of bigger-than-a-handful tits and their rosy tips. Her cunt is hidden beneath the water, just barely, but I catch the very top of her mound and lack of hair. *Does she trim?* Looking higher, I catalog the arch of her brows, her cute nose, and then lower to where the cupid's bow of her plump cherry lips tempts me to bite them. Her.

Slowly, my feet cross into the warm water as this gorgeous creature spreads out her arms and hands, palms facing down, and begins tapping the surface to a synchronized song only she hears. Ripples become slow rolls until a turbulent swirl surrounds her lower half while words form in her mouth. Silently she sways a bit, and a sweet smile graces her lips while the water lights up from within. The rays change from stark white to a soft purple before turning a rich blue and carry through each sequence with gentle ease.

"No." My feet move me back a step and then another, dodging the tendrils of her power that unconsciously reach out for me. It's a caress, this entity with surging emotions that recognizes me for what I am: hers. Her aura calls out for me to come closer—to touch it— but I do the opposite and sidestep its path while walking backward toward the tree that hid my presence. "Goddess, no." *Anything but a sorceress.*

As if it heard my thoughts, the current moves back as if stricken, and guilt settles deep within my gut. This goes against everything that I am—what wolves are taught since we're old enough to understand tradition, pack, and our history.

And while our souls host two entities that make up the whole, the man and wolf, we're not complete without our soul mate. *I could never accept her or her kind.*

My wolf snarls inside my head at that, angry at my refusal to grab our mate, but her nature is something I'll never accept. I'd take a fae, mermaid...fuck, a bloody vampire would've been hard, but I'd agree without a second of hesitation.

Her kind can never be trusted, no matter how utterly perfect I find her.

I could never accept that my mate comes from the same cloth as those who killed my mum.

Once again, the beast snarls, thrashing inside me and my claws burst forth, hair sprouting across my limbs while the crack of bones breaks the silence. He's fighting me for control, something he's never done before—the animal and man are always in sync—but now he's furious.

Slamming a hand against the trunk of the tree, I sink my nails in deep and breathe through the forced mid-shift. Something only the men in my lineage have been able to accomplish; wolf shifters don't walk on two legs, much less forced like this. We let go of our control peacefully to accommodate the other's needs, but never out of ire.

Stand down, I snarl in my mind while my spine curves, forcing me forward. I brace myself as the pain in my chest increases—tearing into the piece of earth with my black-tipped claws and my feet set wide apart.

I'm hurting us both. I know this.

Yet there's no other solution.

I will never love a—

"Son of a bitch." I'm forced to my knees by her essence. Those mystical vines that form who she is—and I've evaded—now have me at their mercy. It sweeps across my still hard cock and strokes, sending electrical pulses from the tip to my heavy balls, and I can't do anything but grit my teeth.

Pleasure ripples through my every nerve ending; I'm at its mercy.

Another tight stroke and purrs start building inside my chest, the sound low and deep. I'm right on the cusp, my muscles tight and jaw clenched when I hear a gasp.

My eyes snap in her direction, and those clear baby blue eyes are my undoing; I come for her. Rope after rope of thick come spurts from the tip and onto the grass below, and all the while I count each rapid rise of her chest and the low moan she emits at the sight of her mate finding pleasure just a few feet away.

I'm not embarrassed by this.

Not one bloody bit.

Because had her kind never killed my mum, I would've worshipped this naughty behavior. Rewarded her after a spanking, turning that perfect arse a nice shade of red. At once my hands clench with the need to touch her, mark her body.

Her queen killed my mother.

That sobering reminder hurts my wolf and he stops his attempt to break free. It also helps me retake my human skin and stand, my eyes on hers the entire time. Not that she tries to stop me.

There's a sadness in her eyes along with acceptance. As if she knows and will not fight me.

Something I appreciate and hate in the same breath. Anger brews within my veins. Her hurt is mine—I feel it deep within my essence —but it's impossible to cover the sun with one finger. I want to tear apart the universe and curse the goddess for the injustice, but nothing will change, and she'll pay for the crimes of the Wiccan royal court.

I'm sorry, Little Moon.

Slipping further into the shadows, I turn toward the tress but then stop. Her voice carries over the breeze, and hearing that sweet little tone is a gift.

"I, Isabella Moore, accept your position."

2
ALPHA
XADIEL

"**F**uck, that last shot hurt," I hiss out a second before the sound of metal clashing fills the air. The brute force vibrates up my arms, shaking my chest, but I keep my stance and push forward with my shoulder. My father grunts as I do, meeting my resistance just as hard, but then a sharp scream rends the air.

Sweat and raindrops roll down my face, the quickly forming bruises from the blunt end of the handle meeting my side during our sparring throb, but I'm quick to turn and listen.

For a few beats there's silence. No one calls for help, and no guard reports a problem.

Not so much as the rustle of leaves, but the moment I retake my fighting position with my chosen weapon, a large sword in my tight grip, another cry rips through the rainy afternoon air, forcing every muscle in my body to tense.

Everyone does.

The sound is full of horror—laced heavily with fear—and the steel drops with a sharp thud against the wet ground. There are a few seconds between the second and next yell, louder and more harrowing, but the person it belongs to is now unmistakable.

Mum, where are you? I ask through the mind link but get nothing. There's a dull static between our communication. It's as if something's preventing her from responding, and for the first time in my life, my heart clenches in fear. *Are you safe?*

Again, I get no response. Nothing.

The one thing shifters in a pack have is the ability to talk through a mental connection, this invisible cord that ties us together and no amount of distance can interrupt. It helps when it comes to protecting the pack or giving out orders, but right now, it's failing me.

It's malfunctioning for my father as well. His worry is palpable and his wolf rises to the surface, eyes becoming black while mine are sure to mimic with their golden tone.

At once, we take off across the training grounds, not wasting another second while every guard on the field begins to shift, the loud cracking of bones following us. Our footfalls sound like thunder snapping against the forest, the horde right behind their leaders while my father's body morphs mid-sprint, his large black wolf snarling as we draw closer to his mate and my mother.

"She's strong and fights better than you, old man." Hearing me, my father's wolf nods to tell me he agrees, but I sense his emotions. His fears. "Our lands are safe. Have faith."

Those words are as much for him as they are for me.

Mum needs us. I can feel it.

And while the bond is different between mother and son, his fury is near choking.

Mates are sacred in our world, and I understand his unease. I'd react the same way if it were mine, and had I found her already, we wouldn't be apart. Ever. That possessiveness and all-consuming need is magnified by the beast within me tenfold.

I grew up watching the love between my parents and the elders all around me. So much of our history and origins start and end with the twining of two souls, the basis of who we are because your other half is both a strength and weakness. Your moral compass and destruction.

One does not function without the other.

We split. Come from both sides. Dad's command comes just as we cross the edge of the field, stepping now into the small patch of untouched forest that separates the royal manor and the training area. *This is my kill. Just get her to safety.*

"No mercy," I say out loud, gaining another nod seconds before he breaks away from the group, taking half our guards with him. *Anyone close to the queen's garden, rush over. Something is wrong.*

I'm patrolling and heard the screams. Heading over, my best friend, Cain, responds quickly. When did he come back from picking up his mate, a she-wolf he met and courted two weeks before completing the bond and moving her to the royal pack from a smaller, northern one? I have no clue, but right now I'm grateful.

He's a top warrior. Trustworthy. Almost as ruthless as I am and will someday take the position of my beta.

My ears twitch after closing the connection, straining to hear any more screams. Instead, I'm met with the heavy steps of wolves running behind me. Their snouts are low to the ground while trying to find a disturbance; a disruption that comes from the direction of my mother's flower garden near the west side of the castle a minute later.

A female figure turns the corner before we do. She's drenched in blood and crying hysterically while looking over her shoulder every few seconds. "Help!"

"What the hell is going on?" I demand, reaching her in a few strides. My hands grip her arms, pulling Aunt Theresa into a hug, trying to calm her enough to talk, but the scent of roses overwhelms me. The blood on her is my mother's. So much of it. "Where is she?"

Warriors surrounds us then, each looking for the enemy, hair bristling while low snarls escape angry jowls. They're feeding off my anger. This live bolt of ire blinds me for a second, and I forget the woman I'm holding is family. My mum's sister.

I feel my claws extend, the breaking of flesh as the talons grow and my fangs descend. Blood drips from my mouth, the sharp teeth breaking through my bottom lip while my grip on her tightens. It's not a full shift, but close enough and the animal in me is snarling and thrashing against my skin, wanting to be let out.

Protect. Kill.

Fury blinds me, annihilating any familial love, and all I see is an enemy.

"Answer me." Each word is spit out from between clenched teeth, the power in me as their next king forcing every wolf to bare its neck. "Now."

"Xadiel, you're hurting me. Let go," Theresa whimpers, her much smaller hands trying to push me away. The stench of her fear infiltrates my senses and my chest expands, taking the acrid scent into my lungs. Right now, I don't care who she is. Mum's blood is all I can see; I don't like the images in my head, made worse by her silence. "Stop this, Nephew."

"Where's my—"

I'm cut off by the sound of a pain-filled howl that for a moment cuts off my senses. Nothing makes sense, and I'm disoriented. Sounds become muffled as my father's cry for his mate fills the air and many others of our pack follow.

Those around me move closer in defense. To protect me.

I drop my hands from Aunt Theresa, dragging my nails down her arms as I stumble back, fingertips now drenched in her life's essence. The force of emotions hits me hard, cutting me bloody deep, but I remain upright.

My mum's sister does fall back, though, scrambling away from me while another wolf flanks her. They're a bit blurry, but enough that I can discern their whereabouts through the sudden fog weighing me down.

Who's the man protecting her? I'm not sure yet, and I don't care.

Not when on my next intake of breath, sound and the control of my movements comes back full force. So do the feelings of wrath and hurt mixed with a need for vengeance that isn't mine, yet I taste it just the same.

I take off toward my father without another word.

All werewolves heed my volatile emotions and stay out of my way, following but at a safer distance. The path that leads to the garden is now crowded with other members of the pack in both forms and all sharing the same expression: devastation.

Each step closer to my family feels like lead. Heavy.

Then there's the trail of blood; the scent of roses permeates the air.

A knot forms in my throat and pain radiates through my limbs, yet I continue toward the two figures on the ground. Tears form in my eyes, but I don't let them fall. My chest feels as though it's caving in on itself, yet I drop beside my father and wrap an arm around him as a broken sob escapes his throat.

My mother is beneath him. His shaking moves her body, and it's then that I take in what they've done.

The queen of werewolves is lifeless and... *motherfuck,* I can't.

What kind of monster does this?

"Who?" The snarled words come through loud and threatening. Kneeling further down, I place my forehead against the back of his neck, trying to give him some support, but he's inconsolable.

To lose your mate is the equivalent of no longer having a heart. Not having a soul.

And as his child, I sense that emptiness. His hurt.

"Xadiel," a male voice says before placing his arm around my shoulder and giving it a squeeze. At once, my face turns and I bare my teeth, hand striking out. My claws dig into the top of Cain's hand on me; he doesn't complain. "Come, my brother. I'll tell you what I know."

"They decapitated her." Voice low, I watch him nod through the dark haze currently over my eyes. "They took her from us."

"I'm so sorry." My friend since childhood swallows hard, chest vibrating as he fights back a howl. There's also a large piece of fabric in his occupied grip, and he bends just enough to lay it respectfully on the ground.

"Who?" Standing, I shrug off his arm and take a protective stance in front of my parents. No one will come near them. No one will take a single step closer unless they want their throat ripped out.

Until I have a killer, everyone's a suspect.

"We don't know how they got onto our lands or who the bastards are."

"They?"

"Yes." He chokes up a bit then. It takes him a minute, but Cain manages to gather his control. The person looking back at me now is a regarded warrior and someone I consider family. *Mum adored him.* That last one stings. Past tense. "We were able to capture one of the two males. Grady has him, along with the two guards who had patrol duties on this side of the property."

"Bring him. I'll deal with the guards after."

"Yes, Alpha." Not the first time someone's called me that, but there's a different connotation this time. The weight comes from the realization that my father will be unable to lead and protect; I'm who they'll come to in times of need, and I'll bear the brunt of the weight without complaint.

This is the least I can do for him while he mourns, and when he's ready, I'll step aside and wait to take the mantle after finding my mate. There's never been a king without a queen. To lead, you must have balance.

I'll deliver the head of this man and anyone else involved on a platter.

That's all that matters.

Vengeance calls to me. Darkness blooms within, and it demands payment.

As Cain leaves, I turn toward the gathered group awaiting instructions. Their attention's already on me. "Everyone, please head home. I'll—"

"Son." That one word stops me, and my head snaps in my father's direction. I also take notice of how his legs shake—of the utter pain in his eyes, and the way he covered Mum's body with the blanket Cain offered. "Please come closer."

I do so without question. There are only a few feet of space between us while my werewolf traits retract—all except for my hands. "Let me take care of everything."

"You make us so proud, Xadiel," he says, voice breaking while his hand rises between us. His nails become claws, tearing the cuticle area. There's also a beat of absolute silence as understanding dawns across our people. No one so much as breathes, but I'm still surprised when he cuts across his chest, fingers digging into the wound before smearing the blood there. "You're going to be the greatest king our people will ever see. So much more than I was, and my father before me."

"Now's not the time. I'll handle everything just the same."

"It is." Again, he swallows hard. "Now kneel."

Every member of our pack falls into position, those in their human skin placing a closed fist over their heart while the wolves lower their faces to rest over their paws.

A show of respect. Acceptance.

I drop to one knee as well. My eyes are on my father; his watery ones are pure black with the presence of his beast.

"I'm ready."

Swallowing hard, my father nods. "Caring for werewolves is what our family was born to do, Xadiel, and I can no longer do that." For a moment he moves his gaze toward those in attendance, an unneeded apology in his expression before refocusing on me. "I'm unable to think past the pain ripping me apart, my son. My world ended today, and a king always puts his people before himself."

With swiftness, he slashes across my pectorals, mixing his sanguine drops with mine. Our combined blood feeds the grass beneath our feet, and the earth shifts a bit as I breathe through the sudden piercing burst of pain and then the power that now flows through my veins.

A vicious growl builds in my chest as little pinpricks rise across my limbs. There's a new consciousness, the awareness of the lives I'll be forever entwined with and responsible for.

Every pack.

Every member and sector leader.

All the lives under my rule.

They're all there. Now a part of my DNA.

"Stand, Xadiel. Rise as the king you were born to be."

3
ALPHA
XADIEL

Howls reverberate throughout the forest and the mental link that connects me to all wolves. It's loud—their cadence full of joy and loyalty—yet there's no evading the heavy undercurrent of pain laced within. Of the heavy grief I'm currently gritting my teeth through as my father tucks the cotton tighter under my mum's body before lifting her into his arms.

He's crumbling before me; his movements are slow while his anguish strikes me with the strength of a whip. I feel it. Everyone. And yet, I swallow my own emotions back while not an ounce of the man who's fought, killed, and ruled our people for centuries remains.

"I'm sorry." Voice hoarse, his orbs flick between black and their natural green tone while the wound on his chest is almost closed. As is mine. "Please forgive me for not staying."

There's so much pain when he meets my eyes, my irises the same golden color as my mum's, and a shuddering breath escapes him. He holds her body a little bit tighter.

"Go on. I'll follow soon." My timbre is gruffer than I intend. Not that he takes offense; Dad simply nods, and I watch with a heavy heart as he heads toward the family mausoleum. It's deep within the property and unavailable to those without familial ties or permission, sitting deep within a cave and carved out of stone.

Crystal stalactites hang at the center near a small opening at the top where water drips down and falls into a pool of crystal-clear water. And surrounding that body of water are tombs, from my great grandfather to now my mother who will find rest within those walls.

Almost there.

I don't acknowledge Cain. Instead, I exhale before addressing those kneeling. "Please stand and go home. I will address everyone later."

"My king, may I speak?" Low, a female's voice comes from the left, and my attention snaps toward her. She's someone I've known all my life. Who's worked with my mum to plan important events or set up accommodations for visitors from outside packs or species.

Her neck is bared to me in a show of respect. Face red from crying.

"Yes, Martina?"

"My...our hearts are with you during this difficult time. We will always love her majesty, and she is missed already." In response, I nod past the lump in my throat, my own eyes misting with tears that will never fall. Everyone has risen and retaken their human skin, nodding in agreement with her sentiment. Nudity isn't a problem among shifters, but those without take what is handed from a member of the guard. Trousers and simple shirts are kept throughout the property and forest. "Please let us help you with all the preparations. Your formal coronation must be held within forty-eight hours after—"

"There will be no festivities. I am your king and don't need to be celebrated."

"Yes, Alpha Xadiel." She looks contrite, ashamed, but she has no reason to be. None of this falls on their shoulders.

"I appreciate the offer, Martina." A small smile is all I can offer her, and she returns it with a watery one of her own. "Don't worry about me, but instead prepare a proper farewell for your queen. Mum loved to eat and dance and run with her people. Send her home to the Moon Goddess with love and peace."

A fancy ball to place a golden crown upon my head means jack shit to me. I'll accept the formality once the cadaver of Mum's killer and all involved lie at my father's feet.

Dead by his hand. Or mine.

My father and people need me to lead, protect, and serve justice. Nothing else matters.

"Of course, King Xadiel. It will be an honor to do so." Nodding, I tilt my head to the side as my ears pick up the rustle of leaves nearby, followed by a few familiar scents and an outsider. The last isn't pack or human, yet the rapid heartbeat and stench of fear is heady. Nearly intoxicating.

More so when a few seconds later the person lands a few steps from me—tossed without care—and on their knees. The frail male cries out from the sudden impact to his legs, and my eyes flick to Cain, who glares at him with so much animosity as realization dawns.

Magic surrounds him, dark and ominous, yet it's clear to me.

Those around us peel their lips back, many taking a step toward the warlock whom I've yet to address, but they stop at my sharp growl.

"Don't."

"This is a mistake." Yet he avoids my eyes. Reeks of fright past the sudden false bravado. He went from a whimper to boredom. "Release me at once or I'll—"

"What is your name, warlock? Who sent you?" I ask, cutting him off. The sharp tendrils of his emotions are clear, almost touchable, and I wonder if anyone else can see this.

Black and serpent-like. Also, dirty.

Then there's the lilt in his accent; it's not natural. He's not English. Of that, I am sure.

Wiccan covens, much like my packs, are based across the world. Yet I'll bet money he's not a native.

"I do not answer to you, mutt."

"Wrong answer." In the blink of an eye, he has a single claw embedded in his cheek, deep enough that a low clicking resounds once the tip taps his teeth. *Tap. Tap. Tap.* "Ready to try again? Nod if you agree, and speak. My patience is nonexistent."

He does and I pull the nail out, smiling as blood seeps from the wound. A few drops splash onto my bare chest, mixing with my sweat. Both roll down my muscles as another light rain descends on us.

Sadness clings to the air; it feels as though the earth mourns our fallen queen.

For a few beats, no one so much as moves, and I count to ten. Each second only serves to further infuriate me.

"Xadiel." At my name, I snap my head past Cain and find my father's beta walking toward me, dragging one of the younger warriors by the hair. My eyes narrow and he swallows hard, loosening his hold just enough that the young man scrambles away but not out of sight. "I'm here to take—"

"Where the fuck have you been, Timoth?" The power in my voice catches him off guard, and so does the anger. He's the second-in-command and should've been here. His job was my mum's protection.

"My apologies, Alpha. I wasn't aware that your father—"

"Where. Were. You? I won't ask again." Beside me, the warlock moves, and a foul smell infiltrates my senses. It pulses, tries to touch me, but can't for some reason. As if there's a wall blocking him. I reward him by stomping on the hand he moves in a circular pattern atop the now dead grass.

Bones crunch under the force, and his magic retreats in terror.

He should fear me. They all should at the moment.

"Fuck," the warlock cries out, and I laugh.

"Do that again, and it'll be your skull the next time." I pat his head with my hand, nails digging into his scalp until the tips are dripping red once again. Only then do I address the royal pack's beta. "Now, Timoth. Answer me."

Just like my father, I'll never condone the mistreatment of a pack member. We don't harm our own without justified cause and proof.

"Your father knew I'd be visiting with family today. I've been back fifteen minutes at the most but ran my usual perimeter check-in with those on duty." He pauses for a moment, and I raise a brow for him to continue. "I'm sorry, my king." An emotion I can't quite decipher flashes across his expression, a mixture of anger and betrayal, and the two make me look closer at the man.

He's the son of a former beta, and his bloodline dates to the first Evergreen monarchy.

He's been my father's right hand for decades, just as his father was before him.

They've been loyal thus far, but that reaction doesn't sit well with me.

Cain will fill that position in due time.

"What are you apologizing for, *Beta*?" I put emphasis on his title on purpose. "Do you have a problem with my father's decision? Do you wish to challenge me?"

Those around us growl at that. Their disapproval is loud and clear.

"Of course not, Alpha. Please don't take my reactions as such." Timoth bares his neck, lowering to his knees. The act appeases my wolf and he calms a bit, accepting the respect. "I'm upset because I failed our queen. Had I not taken the time off today, our luna would be—"

"Good." I cut him off. Nothing he says changes anything. His posture loses some of its rigidness, though, and that also won't last long. My next words aren't just for him, but for all my people. "Because I'd hate to kill someone my parents care about. Understood?"

A challenge is only over once an opponent is dead.

No tapping out. No mercy.

"Yes, Alpha."

"Now finish answering the question."

Timoth's eyes flick to the guard who grows more pallid under his glare. "It's normal for me to make rounds with those on shift, and all units responded but him. His supervisor even tried, and after no response, we headed to his post. I found him mid-escape, past our southern borders, and with a dead Armand close to his location."

"I see." For the briefest moment, my eyes close. Another family member, my uncle, is gone. Aunt Theresa lost her sister and mate. *Bloody hell.* The ache in my chest intensifies, hurt radiating down to my bones, but I rein all emotions in. They need a leader. My family deserves justice.

"NO!" a female voice cries out then, and I know it's my aunt. There's pain and despair, and her wails grow in volume. There's also the sound of thrashing in someone's hold, her warning growls coming out near acerbic, yet her eyes are on me when mine snap open. "He's lying, Nephew! Tell me he's lying!"

"Is Armand dead, Timoth?"

"I'm sorry." That's his response, and it's a shot to my gut to watch my aunt dissolve into nothing. Her limbs go weak. Her tears are a torrent as they soak Martina's dress as the latter wraps her arms around her.

"Kill him, Nephew. Or let me." A whispered request, and I don't respond.

There will be no judgement until the truth is uncovered.

"Come here, pup." My fangs drop, and I pin him with a cold glare. The guard, while in his twenties, is still a kid compared to my ninety. A werewolf's life expectancy is long; most die of old age or from not surpassing the death of a mate.

Those bonds are our biggest weakness. That, and silver.

Slowly, he stands on shaky legs and walks over. His posture is one of defeat while the heady scent of panic becomes prominent.

He stops a few feet from me. "Yes, Alpha?"

"Is he lying, Luke?"

"No." It leaves him on a whimper, and those gathered snarl. His body shakes at that while the wolf within submits.

Taking in a deep breath, I let it out slowly, hands clenching and unclenching. "Did you help them kill your queen? My uncle?"

"Yes." A nervous twitch. There's also the heavy cloak of shame.

"Why?"

"I had no choice, Alpha. He threatened to kill my—" Blood gurgles out of the wound, the single strike from my hand breaking his neck while my talons sliced him open from one side to the other. He never had the chance to see the move, much less anticipate how quick I truly am.

"There is always a choice, and it's to never betray your pack." A thud greets my ears a second later as Luke's body meets the ground, and I turn my attention to Timoth. My closed fist bangs on my chest, my appreciation clear. "Thank you, Beta." *Take my aunt inside and request the healer come at once. She'll need something to help her rest.*

"Always, King Xadiel." *Anything you need, I'm here for your family.* The beta quickly lifts my catatonic aunt into his arms and carries her toward the main house. All that's left of her are the silent tears of heartbreak.

Once they're out of sight, I turn to the warlock, who's been watching me. Tracking my every move. He's been smart enough not to try and conjure anything again, and my smile is in condescending

22

appreciation. I also toss at his face a piece of Luke's throat caught on a nail.

"Let's try that again, shall we? Name?"

"Let me go. You'll never see me again." Now he's meek. No more backbone.

"No." This time, I circle him while the frail man trembles. His robe is long, yet it doesn't hide the puddle of piss currently growing beneath him. Then, there's the acrid stench of his magic mixed with distress which grows, and I inhale deeply, taking it deep into my lungs.

My wolf likes it. Relishes in his panic.

This man has no idea what real pain looks like, but he will.

I'm going to drain him slowly. A cut at a time. A chunk of flesh with each strike.

"Please, Alpha. I've been forced to—*fuck!*" he yells out, using his still useful hand to cover the hole left behind by my nails on his chest. Blood seeps from between his fingers at a rapid pace. "I-It's Tonio Salicio."

"And who sent you here, Tonio Salicio?"

"I'll never betray my true mistress. She saved me once."

"Suit yourself." In the blink of an eye, I have his throat in my hold—fingers wrapped tightly—and begin to apply pressure. His feet are off the ground, the fingers of his good hand trying to pry mine off, but that stops the second I punch through his ribs.

A scream rips through the air while his skin and bones give way, tearing under the strength of my fist. I come out through the back, stretching my digits out before exiting with a chunk of flesh in my palm.

"Stop!"

"Who is your mistress?"

"I can't...figlio di puttana!" *So he's Italian, but from which coven?* The Wiccan royals are allies, their queen a friend of my mum, and she'll be furious. They will understand why I've killed him.

"Interesting choice of words." The next strike is to his shoulder and then collarbone, ripping a chunk out each time and then tossing them onto Luke's dead body. Another on his right thigh, and then left. "Ready to talk?"

The man is a mess, his tears mixing with snot and the sanguine rush of his wounds. From head to toe, I mutilate him a piece at a time while pulling a louder cry from his chapped lips. I want everyone to hear his pain. Relish in it the way my animal and I have.

"No more."

"Her. Name." The tip of a black-tipped claw rips his robe and flesh from belly button to sternum. Not deep enough to kill, but I'm sure it burns like a bitch. "Tell me, and I'll put an end to your suffering."

"Leonora Moore."

"Liar," I hiss out from between clenched teeth; a fury so strong rips through me, and my muscles expand. My teeth are at his throat before the arsehole takes in a pain-filled breath. I'm breaking the skin, grazing his jugular before pausing. "Tell me the truth. Who fucking sent you."

"Leonora sent me." Tonio coughs, reddish spittle flying out, and I pierce a little deeper. In his blood I taste the darkness of his heart; the magic in his veins is tainted. "The Moores want to eliminate whom they perceive as threats, and your kind are the biggest targets at the moment."

Betrayal cuts deep. It weighs heavily on my heart.

Yet what I focus on is the grief of losing two loved ones.

Before he can utter another word, I've ripped out his throat and tossed his mangled body atop Luke's. Two traitors. Two worthless bastards.

Blood drips from my mouth as I turn to face my people, teeth red and my wolf present in my eyes. We're one at the moment, completely in sync, and I spit the remnants of Tonio's trachea on the ground.

"No Wiccan descendant will ever be allowed on our sacred lands again. No matter the sex or age, kill them on site." The ground shakes at the decree, feet stomping while the air cracks from the sound of closed fists pounding on their chests. "We're at war with the witches, my pack, and I'll never rest until Leonora Moore's head sits atop a spike at our borders. And if her family intervenes, they'll be gifted the same fate. No mercy."

"No mercy," they recite back in unison.

This pain in indescribable. My father is inconsolable. Yet I'll lead them through this, and only in the aftermath of our revenge will I allow my own pain to surface.

That's a lesson I learned today from a man who lost it all.

A king always put his people before himself.

4
Isabella

He's beautiful. Every animalistic inch of him has been sculpted by the gods to perfection. The literal definition of chiseled muscles, a sharp jaw, and the soulful golden eyes of a powerful beast.

My mate is tall. At the very least, he's two feet taller than me, and that's in human form.

But his animal...

Goddess, he's perfection.

And for those few glorious moments, I allowed myself the gift of meeting his stare. I'd been mesmerized—owned by a secretly woven spell that robbed me of breath and function. My skin prickled with awareness and my nipples tightened to near painful tips; he caused a heated throb between my thighs I've never experienced before.

Just like I knew he'd find me. Felt the moment he entered the woods and the tremors of his thundering steps the closer to me he came. Because every being walking this earth has a vibration they emit, a low pulse that thrums, and while I ignore most, his is undeniable. It slithers across my flesh, striking with pleasure, and mine returned the favor.

The magic that's an extension of me couldn't be held back. It feeds off my desires—hunger.

I want him. My mate.

Patience, Isabella. He's been lied to.

This I know, too. Politics and manipulation have led us here from all sides, and I've come to accept that our path together has many twists and turns that will span a century.

Exhaling, I count to fifty while closing my eyes. His essence is all around me, and the scent of his spend and the cedar with a hint of mint coming from his skin embeds itself deep, merging with my soul. It brings with it a sense of home and belonging that can only be provided by your other half.

Because a soul mate is sacred. Above everything.

There is only one soul bond during our lifetime, and it's meant to be cherished. No one can love, understand, and make you stronger while also humbling you as they can. It's overwhelming, this sudden urge to be near him, yet the moment our eyes met, life truly began and my past is nothing but a distant memory.

He makes me whole. Lessens the weight of my burden while simultaneously breaking me.

However, I don't begrudge him the tumultuous emotions wrecking his heart: hate, need, and revenge is all he's known for a long time.

The time will come to help him. The stars will show me the way.

Because I've dreamt of this meeting for two summers now. Kept my visions and warnings to myself while preparing my heart for the inevitable.

A seer is just as prone to heartache as anyone else. Seeing it beforehand doesn't change the outcome, and the universe has a way of righting itself; a path can never deviate. The end will always be the same.

Just like I couldn't save my parents, no matter how much I wish I could.

Another deep inhale and a shiver rushes up my spine, forcing my attention away from painful thoughts and back to the man who possesses my soul. The tug in my chest is also harder. Sharper and alert.

He's still here. Watching me.

My blue eyes snap open and my head tilts, catching the sharp glow of gold a second before they darken. Swirls of darkness mix with the aurum, the colors swirling while a low rumble greets my ears.

No words. Just a soothing purr that settles the pain he's caused.

As if he has no choice but to comfort me.

The water lapping at my flesh feels like a caress the longer he stares. As if the drops of come that fell from his thick shaft, painting the grass below his clawed feet, are marking my flesh.

It's time to go.

"Goodbye." The lone word slips past my lips on a whisper. It's so low he almost doesn't hear, but then I'm met with the angry growl of a wolf, and that settles my heart.

The man might not be ready for me, but his animal is. His displeasure is palpable, yet neither make a move to stop me.

And without looking back, I turn and wade toward the shore. My siblings are not far from here, sleeping and resting after a long day and the bad news received, unaware of my sneaking out. We've traveled far to escape those who killed our family and the vampire king, but the time of our return draws near.

You can't outrun fate.

The sanctified lands my family owns a few miles away is on neutral ground, yet the protection spells keep us unseen. Undetectable to our kind or other species unless we invite you inside.

We're far enough that those hunting the Moore heirs haven't reached the soil we rest upon.

Close enough to those that see us as enemies for reasons that are untrue and unjust. Father never spoke of the reasons why—never an ill word toward those who hate us—but instead, promised me it would all work out before I understood how deep the lies ran.

It wasn't until my first dream that I realized how steep my hill would be. Hurts my soul.

Moreover, if my siblings were to wake and find me gone, they'd freak out.

But tonight, I had no choice.

The stars don't lie. Neither does the moon.

Before we return to the Moore home, we had to meet. The seedling of doubt in his heart had to be created.

Until we meet again, my heart.

I'M LAYING DOWN INSIDE OUR PRIVATE QUARTERS AFTER A FEW DAYS of traveling by boat, while my siblings have dinner in another locomotive cart. We're on our way to Naples after traveling for days from England to Italy, something I am finding bittersweet.

I left my heart back in that forest.

Returning is inevitable for me, but so is the future full of hurt that awaits. Even if at the end I walk away, my mate needs to see the truth for himself. I'm going to take away his burden—that choking pain crushing his soul—and then he will choose.

Two paths. One answer. A swinging pendulum.

A loud snore from one of the guards traveling with us pulls me out of my thoughts. Coming from the cabin near the back end, I can make out the grunting sound that ends with the smacking of lips and then the low chuckles of his brethren.

The mixture of sounds makes me snort, and I'm glad no one is here to hear me.

But then that amusement dies when reality hits me in the chest again.

I'm alone. Heartbroken.

There's also so much I want to say and can't. Every time I close my eyes, I'm haunted by the past and future—the silent rejection that slowly tears at my heart. This time he was unable to say the words, but the next...

"Things will work out. I vow to make it so for all of us." A tear slips from the corner of my eye and I wipe it away, glad that my siblings aren't here to witness this moment of weakness. I don't want them to worry or carry more weight than what's already on their shoulders. This is my burden. He is mine. "The road to happiness is paved by tears."

A saying that accompanies me through the darkest moment.

Since the first time I dreamt of *him*.

Yet it also reminds me that the alternative would be permanent. Sorrow is unavoidable; our mates are the key, but it won't be easy. I'll lose my sister, but her mate will bring her back—her vampire will face death himself for the right to love her, and he will win.

Gabriella's path will be easier than mine when it comes to her mate's acceptance, but her path is not less painful. Life gives and takes. The gods bless and then destroy you on their next breath to appease their plans.

I'm cursed with knowing every outcome and not being able to stop the bleeding before it starts. It's why our parents gave up their lives, because if Gabriella intervened, there would be no rebirth for her. Leo would never ascend to the crown.

Witches all around the world would be hunted down until only I remained chained and enslaved by another power-thirsty king, and his son.

Many are threatened by her gifts.

Others fear how strong the young Moore warlock will be.

Heavy is the head, but sharp are the blades.

Nothing changes the outcome, no matter how much I wish it were different; our paths were set in stone the moment our lungs took in their first breath. Many have tried and failed, and the witches working with the enemy to block my gifts—seeing their next move —isn't enough to stop me.

Even muddled, I understand. Not with the kind of abilities that thrum through our veins, and the heavy crown laden with thorns that sits atop our heads.

A family given a gift. A lineage burdened by suffering and betrayal.

Greed. Power. Blood.

Gabriella is the mistress of death, while I see the lies and deceit hidden behind veils of love.

I couldn't save our parents. I can't save her.

"We're back," Gabriella calls out then, entering our cabin with what looks to be a pastry in her hand and a tea for me. She eyes me, brows furrowing, but doesn't ask any questions while our little brother closes our door. He's not paying attention to me, currently heading for the bed I made for him. "We brought you back a little snack. It'll be a while before we make it to Naples...you should eat."

"Later. Too tired to eat." *Lies.* More like my mind can't find rest.

"Thought you'd be sleeping. Did you—" The shaking of my head cuts her question off. *You okay?* she mouths, and I nod. "Need help to fall asleep?"

"Please."

"One dormire special coming up."

"Dork." At that, she sticks her tongue out while I watch her grab one of the two small bags she brought with her. This one has a few dried herbs, valerian being one of them. From here I can scent the calming touch of chamomile, but with the added root, I'll more than likely fall deep.

Mom would make me a tea just like this whenever my dreams or visions kept me up.

A pang of grief makes my eyes mist, but I blink them back while turning my face from hers. Instead, I focus on Leo, who's already asleep and how a few second later mimics the high snore of our guards.

It's loud and accompanied by a whistle that makes him wake up, look around, and then promptly fall back asleep. Gods, it's hard, but I cover my mouth with a hand while my eyes automatically meet Gabriella's. She's biting her bottom lip, shoulders shaking, and still a tiny giggle escapes her.

Then we're both cracking up.

Clutching our stomachs and trying to bite back the laughter. Wiping our cheeks as a few tears escape and still, our brother is none the wiser. The kid sleeps like the dead. The loud dead.

"Gods, I needed that," Gabby snickers, shaking her head before dropping the now pouched dried herb to let steep. There's a low incantation from her lips, the words we've heard thousands of times, before she gives me a wink. "Been a while since we've had a real reason to laugh."

"Very true." Taking the offered cup, I take a sip and hum. Just like Mom's. And while valerian isn't known to be the best smelling or sweetest taste, the small spell makes it so. Almost like a dessert, fresh and light with a hint of apples in the note. "Feels good to forget, if even for a moment."

"Talk to me, Sister. What do you see?"

"A lot, more than I'd like, but now isn't the time." Then I give her our sign: one nod for bad news and two nods for a clear passage.

Tonight, she gets two even though it's a lie. It's the least I can do.

I'll let her find rest before her world implodes.

5
Isabella

"What is it?" Gabriella asks after we step outside and onto an empty caboose with a glass windowpane door. The space is just large enough for us to keep an eye on our cabin and within reach, in seconds, if the need arose. Then there's the vast city and landscape to our left, beautiful and calm, yet it'll be dulled by what I have to say.

"We're walking into a bloodbath," I say, keeping my voice even, although a harsh shiver still runs through me. My grip on the handrail turns my knuckles white. "The vampires are getting closer."

"There's something else, isn't there?" Gabriella has every right to her trepidation. To the worry.

"My sight is being shielded, but yes." It's been happening since our parents were killed. Anything to do with those responsible becomes muddled, yet this is clear. Meeting the vampire king is her destiny. "Your path is intertwined with his, Gabby."

No need to explain who the "he" is. Yet she still lets out a choked gasp, her face losing a little of its rosy color. "How can this be?"

"Which one?" He's going to make you so happy.

"Both."

In response, I shrug, going for nonchalance. Our connection as twins lets her feel my emotions and right now, worry is the dominant one. "My guess is a powerful witch, but not stronger than the Moore bloodline. I'll break whatever they've cast."

She nods. "What's his plan, though? Why does the king of vampires need a sorceress?"

"Sadly, you'll ask him personally soon enough." Because he's your mate.

"How much of a window, Sister?" Gabby shifts her weight from foot to foot. Clenches and unclenches her fists. "Do we have time to get Leo to Uncle Roberto's?"

"Three moons."

"Are you sure? You just said you can't see as clear—"

"The path might change, but the destination doesn't. Fate is a determined bitch."

"You have that faraway look again, Isa. Another vision?" my brother asks a few hours later, effectively pulling me from replaying the conversation I had with Gabriella. I hate what's ahead and how soon it will all fall apart for us. How out of control it all feels. "Is something wrong?"

It's not, but there will be. "Just lost in thought, kid."

"Promise?"

"I do."

We're in our uncle's backyard, side by side after a heavy meal, and a few feet away from where Gabriella has decided to take her respite. She's always found peace outdoors while sitting beneath a tree with her fingers embedded deep in the soil. Nature breathes and she exhales, keeping the balance between life and death.

It's how I found her the night our parents were murdered. The same serene expression on her face, completely oblivious to the horrors happening inside the manor we've called home all our lives.

I will never look at that house the same way again. No warmth. No peace.

"And you? Are you okay staying here?" Lifting a hand, I ruffle his hair and watch the annoyance flash across his features. At thirteen summers, the future king is easy to annoy, and as his older sister, I've earned the right to give him a tough time. To bug and be playful and ease him into his role as a leader someday, but for now, we must leave him here.

I hate it. Abhor the emotions being inside our uncle's property have brought forth in me.

I'm not one to harbor hate or dark emotions, but this I can't fight. The man abandoned us after his brother's murder. Betrayed his king.

But for now, he'll be useful. Father wanted Leo here, and I'll abide while biting my tongue.

Their reckoning will come.

"The moment I take the throne, I'm making you eat a toad." Leo's words snap me from my thoughts, and I laugh, shoulders shaking. "Just wait and see."

"What if I made you eat one now?"

"One day, Isa. One day." His face scrunches in repulsion, the same reaction as Dad whenever Mom cut off his caffeine consumption. "Just nasty."

A giggle escapes from me. "I'm sure you'll try."

"Just remember one day I'll be king. Payback." Leo becomes quiet after that, no more teasing, and the expression on his face saddens me. Exhaling, the weight on his shoulders makes him appear older than he is. "Honestly, I'd rather be home, but I understand, and promise to behave. I'll be fine here."

"I'm proud of you." Movement catches my attention from the corner of my eye; Uncle Roberto stands near us, and I give him a small nod. "Why don't you head inside and see if Aunt Silla needs help? She still might have some bombolone Gabby didn't snatch up."

Before the last word leaves me, Leo is racing inside while the presence of our zio comes closer. He stops at the other side of me. Quiet and pensive, Roberto looks out toward my sister while I study his expression.

Regret. Abject misery.

"You hate me." Not a question.

"I do." Won't sugarcoat it or calm his guilty conscience. "And while we both have burdens to carry, I faced their anger and helped shoulder the pain while you hid, Uncle. You left us to fend for ourselves after years of feigning love and fealty to the royal family— to your brother and king."

That cuts him. His face snaps toward me, pinched tight and with watery eyes. "That allegiance cost me my only sibling, Isa. I'm ashamed, not guilty."

Shame. Another emotion I'm all too familiar with.

It hurts to know you couldn't save someone you love. That you let them down.

"Father, please. It's not too late," I plead, holding my hand out toward him and Mom. Begging them to come with us. *"There must be a way to stop this. Something we've missed."*

"You can't outrun fate, Isabella. You know this." And I do, but I also can't accept it. That there will be a world where they no longer exist. *"Daughter, you've seen what I've seen and the end for those involved. Never falter, sweet child. You three are our future, and many will depend on you."*

"But we *need you."*

"Baby, please go." Mom looks at me with tears in her eyes while my younger brother trembles and the sound of something

being slammed against our front door grows louder. The walls shake, the clash of fighting outside unmistakable; there are two guards on duty tonight, as is customary. Father has never been one for keeping families apart at night, and if you work for our royal court, you're expected to break bread with your wife and child. "Get Leo out of here. You three are our future, Isa. Save our people."

Dad lowers his face toward Leo and lays his forehead over his. There's a whispered exchange between them, tears streaming down both faces, but I can't make out what he says. Yet the moment Dad's radiant pulse begins to flow, I throw my arms around Mom and cry. It's something he's done in the past with all of us after a scare or learning a new spell, and in moments of excitement and fear, he soothes with the low frequency that wraps around us with love.

Yet today, it hurts.

I sob because I'll never see them again. Not in the flesh.

No more hugs. No more late-night talks and lessons.

The scent of patchouli and lavender will fade with time and never come back.

"I love you, Mom." The choked words are full of sorrow, the reality tearing me apart. "By blood and pact."

"We are one, Isabella."

"I'll make you proud." Another harsh blow to the front entrance has us pulling apart, my eyes flashing to Dad. "Keep them safe."

"Even if it means someday they'll hate me, I'll push them in the right direction."

"And we'll always be with you." Quickly, he pulls me in for a hug. Strong and tight, but broken when the front door to our family home splinters open, the thick wooden pieces slamming against walls. Glass breaks, the sound carrying all the way to his office where we stand. "Never doubt that, my children. Your mother and I will watch over and help guide you three."

"Why?" That's what eats at me. Roberto told the Rossi family we'd be home and where their leaders would await their fate; just like Father asked him to. The man set up his own death on his terms knowing—seeing—the best outcome for us.

We shared the same gift, even if his was tactile. Hugging his brother gave him the answers needed.

And for some reason, Father was also able to hide the fact from me until after.

Once on the run, I witnessed the devastation on our uncle's face in a vision. Saw him set up what looked like the betrayal to his brother and brethren in a vision, one where our guards should've been shown mercy. That was the agreement; only the King and Queen Moore were to be harmed, yet two of our men died that day.

Women lost a brother or father and a son along with their leaders.

And all to save the Moore children. To ensure the survival of our people.

He lets out a heavy and agony-filled sigh, one of his hands rubbing the back of his neck. His stare also evades mine now, a sign he's uncomfortable. "I don't think this will give you the—"

"Let me worry about what I need or don't need. Just answer, please."

Another rough exhale, and his shoulders drop. "The Rossi and Mariano men had plans for you and your sister, Isabella. Paolo..." at his only sibling's name, he chokes a bit "...he saw you both broken, bound, and used as pawns to kill—"

"The fae king," I finish for him because those covens rose against us with the backing of powerful magic, yet they failed to see the blackness in the fae king's heart. That he'd betray them before our mates joined the fight, and he has. *I'm the one Larue wants.* "One of the three families, the Salicios fell under Larue's blade, all but a handful he kept to aide him, while the others to the wrath of the vampire."

"Correct. This was—"

"Father's doing."

"Yes. He trusts *King Astor* but I—"

"Have no say when it comes to our mates." I don't miss the

HALF TRUTHS: THEN

venom in his tone when speaking of Gabriella's mate. *What will he say when he meets mine?* Because that's the one thing he agreed with, swore about, to those involved within the revolt. How he won their trust. *Disgusting pigs, all of them.* The intermingling of our bloodline with that of wolf and vampire will cause an uproar between all species, but hate will never win. Never does, because love is love and fuck anyone who thinks differently. "It's best you learn that and quickly, Uncle. Intervene, and it won't be the men you should fear but your own bloodline."

Just the thought brings forth fire to my veins, and I recant *veni ad me* while my hand opens and fingers curl as Gabriella taught me. I can't give and take a life, but making you feel a little of that pain and loss is different. The action catches him off guard; he pales and slams a hand on his chest while I watch.

Calm. Unaffected. Morbidly.

His life's essence heeds my call and shifts, the small bit of aura dancing toward me.

I won't deny that the sensation is thrilling, and a higher under-standing of my sister blooms.

"Isabella," he groans, his thin form shaking. "Please stop."

"*Prohibere.*" At once, the grip I had vanished and he drops, a gasp leaving him. I kneel with him, and with the tip of two fingers raise his eyes to meet mine. "What you did was follow a direct order from your king. I'll forgive you for that, but abandoning us is an offense I won't overlook. You failed your brother by not helping us escape and hide, by ignoring the call to lay him and your sister-in-law to their honorable rest. *Disgraceful.*"

"I love you three as if you were mine."

"Yet you closed your mouth and turned your back." Leaning forward, I kiss his forehead. "Someday you will make amends, but not today. Not for a while."

"Will you ever forgive me? Will Gabriella?" Roberto asks, his expression a sad mixture of culpability and despair. "Can I regain your trust in me?"

39

"Protect Leo with your life, Uncle." That's the best I can give him. The wounds are still too raw, the memories haunting me. "Don't make me hurt you because I will not hesitate to protect my siblings and their mates."

I let that threat stand. I know his position, and now he knows mine.

Because I've seen his reaction when both men come forward.

Two beasts. Mortal enemies.

A vampire. A werewolf.

Both kings.

And more importantly, I will kill for them when the time comes.

6
ALPHA
XADIEL

N ot rejection, but *position*.

I can't get her bloody response out of my head. My mate's reaction to a clear rejection, although I never spoke the ancient words to break our small bond. *I don't want to hurt her.* Yet emotionally I am, and it goes against everything I am as a werewolf and man.

Soul mates are sacred. A gift from the moon goddess herself.

What's more, those few minutes fortified the tethers created by her scent, what drew me to that lake and then to recognize her as mine while my mind revolts against our wrongful pairing. Our rela-

41

tionship can't move forward even if I recognize the beautiful girl as mine, making the witch's reaction a punishing reel while the animal within me growls under my skin; his anger as palpable as is his yearning.

He doesn't see the familial resemblance to the woman who killed Mum.

Not the blood ties or the possibility she's involved.

None of this matters to him. How every investigation about her comes back empty—Gabriella and Isabella were kept a mystery to many. Never seen by anyone outside their coven or their most trusted allies, and my Mum was one of those people.

What are they hiding? It's driving me bloody fucking insane.

Her appearance here does answer one question: where they've been.

My men hadn't been able to locate them. They were smart to conceal themselves under the enemy's nose, I'll give them that.

I hate her family. Want her parents' blood on my muzzle, dripping down my fangs.

The beast doesn't care, though, and craves his mate—his female —while I abhor who and what she is.

Our needs have never been so out of sync. I'm torn in two. A witch has no place in my kingdom, much less as my luna, and more so when her last name is Moore.

And yet, I can't stop thinking about her. Wanting. Craving. Throbbing.

Yearning for the scent of jasmine's to infiltrate my senses. Looking for her each night as I revisit the lake in hopes of seeing my little moon. It's a blooming tick that controls me, growing with each passing day, and I'm near the point of hunting her down even if it's to steal a bloody taste.

To feel her pinned beneath me, her cunt choking my cock, even if it's just once.

A sharp yelp of pain followed by the snap of bones pulls me from my thoughts and back to the fight happening mere steps from me.

The challenger is a lower-ranking warrior who wishes to move up to patrol supervisor, and his attempt to do so is piss-poor at best.

"Yield," my gamma snarls. He has him on the floor with an arm pulled back, elbow and forearm visibly broken and with his fangs at the man's neck. The pain and acknowledgement of his superior's command has his body turning. His fur recedes and his dirty, bloodied skin appears with deep bruises littering the flesh.

Next is the realigning of bones. They snap in place, all but the broken one, while his snout pulls back, revealing a pained expression and busted lip. "No more."

Cain stands then and gives the two enforcers standing at the ready a nod. They're quick to remove the whimpering shifter, heading straight for the healer while my gamma takes a small towel from his mate.

At once, she begins to check him for injuries. It's subtle, a quick roam of the eyes, but I take in their interaction while swallowing back my emotions. I'm not ready to acknowledge them or her.

And for the first time in my life, I'm jealous. A bit bitter.

My little witch will never have the chance to do the same. Fawn over me after a challenge or battle.

"Satisfied, love?"

"Shut it, you." No real anger, more like embarrassment if the touch of pink across his mate's cheek is anything to go by. "Besides, we have more pressing things to..."

I tune out the rest while surveying the warriors still waiting in formation. The vast training grounds are set up to fight in both skins, human and fur, while the large forest beyond remains untouched.

Sacred.

The Evergreen Pack lands are over two hundred and twenty square miles wide with an English castle at the center surrounded by smaller mansions where unmated wolves and guests find accommodations. That large manor is where the werewolf royal family has lived for generations, and with each ruling alpha serving his people for two centuries at the very minimum.

My father was the last king and remained so for three centuries, the longest reign before stepping aside and naming me his successor. After the exchange of power, one of the pack leaders from across the pond stepped forward to challenge the decision—a tosser that bared his neck after the first swipe of my clawed hand across his underbelly.

No other alpha or wolf made a sound. Every single one accepted and pledged allegiance to the werewolf throne.

However, she-wolves *will* challenge her.

A thought that angers me, and an angry roar slips through my lips. "Shift."

"Yes, Alpha." One by one the warriors begin to turn, the group of a hundred in attendance shedding their humanity for their beasts. These are my top two groups of fighters and leaders of my army, the most lethal being the elite ten which my gamma trains privately.

The rest rotate schedules, training in smaller clusters while switching guarding posts with each other with two days off in between every forty-eight-hour shift.

Trespassers near the main entrance—a witch and a warlock. They're heading toward neutral grounds. Need backup.

Beta Timoth's mind link makes me pause, eyes flicking to Cain. His posture is defensive, placing himself between his mate and an invisible threat. He also heard the call, all our fighters have, and I hold up a single finger.

We're coming. Capture, but don't kill, I respond to Timoth through a separate link. Private.

Are you sure?

Never question me, Beta.

My apologies, my King.

"First group will be accompanying us." At my orders, the elite fall into a formation a few feet from me: tall, proud, and ready to defend. "All others will protect our perimeters and not move until I call you home. We're on lockdown. Understood?"

"Yes, Alpha."

With that I take off, shifting mid-sprint while the thunderous sounds of paws meeting the grassy fields grow louder. Angrier. No one here has forgotten what the Moore matriarch took from us, and by default, her kind is despised.

She's been untouchable and under the king's protection since then, but that won't last forever. Moreover, within reason or not, I've killed more than a few witches over the last twelve months.

What will Isabella think? My heart clenches at the thought. At the knowledge that she'll hate me—curse our bond—the day I tear out the heart of the woman who gave her life. The pain is sharp. *It won't change a thing, though.*

I'm owed my pound of flesh. Revenge.

After the murder of my mum, we hunted those sects residing in England. Most were wise to flee the country, but the first casualties were a smaller coven of females that foraged too close to our borders, seeking a certain plant cultivated by the lake where I met Isabella.

Were they good people? No. Of this, I'm certain as their aura matched that of the male witch from a year ago. Dark and ominous, and when I found them taking enough wolfsbane to kill many of my kind, I tore out their hearts without a second of remorse.

But today it could be Isabella near the borders. What if she gets hurt?

The beast pushes me further back, taking full control in a blind rage of panic. We push past everyone, creating enough distance between us that I reach the tree line and take the first left toward my kingdom's entrance. Not even Cain, who's the second fastest, can keep up.

Trees begin to blur, blending into the background in hues of green and brown while the sunlight filters through pockets in between branches. My sharp claws scrape against the ground as I push myself faster, dodging any root or obstacle in my way. Those following have also picked up the pace, and before long I cross over the private passageway many don't know about.

Almost there, Beta.

It leads me to the entrance but from the left, hidden behind a large statue of our first king while his luna is on the opposite side of the now open-wide iron gate. Large, the heavy stone monument shields me from view, and I slow down.

Timoth is standing guard over a man in a red robe no more than thirty feet from me, snarling while rogues surround him. Neutral grounds are just beyond the next tree line.

Instantly, my worry over Isabella boils into a merciless rage at the sight of the six frothing-at-the-mouth mutts. These wolves are scum, a stain on our society—criminals that committed sins against their pack—and were exiled by those in charge or sentenced by my father during his time on the throne.

Because very few chose to live as loners. Shifters need familial connections and thrive in groups, and these animals here are not the peaceful kind that decided living among humans is what they need —prefer.

No. The six arseholes crouched and poised, ready to attack, are volatile.

Bloodshot eyes, matted hair, and thin frames full of battle scars.

Then, there is the hate in their stares, and the intent to kill to protect the warlock is clear.

They also haven't noticed my presence, much less the gathering horde behind me.

My paw taps the ground twice, and Timoth's head snaps up. His shoulders relax a bit.

Kill them all but the warlock, I snarl through the link, rushing at the one who chooses to launch himself at my beta. Our bodies collide, my much larger black wolf slamming into the muddy brown pelt where his ribs are, and the impact disorients him. There's the crack of his bones and a pain-filled yelp, but I don't give him the chance to gather himself.

Within seconds, my teeth are at his neck and I snap it like a twig.

Others around me join, the growls and snarls filling the air. From the corner of my eye, I catch Cain swiping his paw across an under-belly and then the quick gush of blood that sprays his face. The tan wolf cries and falls, whimpering and dragging himself away, but my gamma doesn't give him the chance.

The scrawny wolf lies limp with a ripped throat before his next intake of breath.

The rest fall just the same. All except one.

He bursts through the cluster of ash trees across from us, teeth bared and heading straight for me. The wolf is small, malnutrition noticeable, and I stop him with a singular growl. "Shift."

A sharp yelp escapes his snout, paws coming to swipe across his nose while he rubs the side against the grass. He's fighting the command, trying to regain his footing, but nature is unforgiving. The body responds without his input, forcing the transformation, and what's left a minute after is nothing more than a pup.

The kid can't be any older than seventeen and looks to need medical attention with cuts and bruises littering his human skin. He also appears to be under the influence of some kind of spell.

"Please make it stop," his voice cries out hoarsely, and hands scratch at his ears. They're also bloodied, the torn dermis infected.

"Pin him." Cain jumps on him, holding the kid down at once while I turn my attention to the warlock. There is a repetitive incantation coming from him, the pupils of his eyes blown wide, but I stop him with one swift kick to his exposed knee.

It breaks, and so does his hold on the kid.

Both scream, one in pain and the other in fear, the latter of which calms when he sees me.

The teenager bares his neck and stills.

Not the act of a dangerous rogue. Even the peaceful ones who leave their packs for a solitary life among humans, no malice in their hearts, become unattached to their roots.

Customs.

Not out of disrespect; they're polite and peaceful, but more so out of losing their connection to the animal. The wolf hides. Withdraws.

The dangerous rogue, though, is just a bloodthirsty arsehole. Provoking, fighting, and killing is their nature.

Are you thinking what I am?

Help him. Then, a barely perceptive nod is all I give Cain. He'll know what to do.

My focus is on the gasping bloke squirming under Timoth. There's also the real lack of restraint or acknowledgment of the spell, but before I can ask my beta, he shakes his head.

A warning growl rips from him, and his hands wrap around the warlock's neck. "What did you do to me? Where's the blonde woman that I saw with you?"

It's not Isabella. Her red hair is unmistakable and so is my relief.

I'm not ready to see her. Or deal with what we are...not until I kill all involved.

"Afraid, puppet?" Timoth tightens his grip, the man's face turning red. His lips are a little blue, yet his speech is clear. "We're coming for every last one of you."

"I'm going to enjoy ripping you—"

"Stop."

"My king?" Timoth grits out. Angry.

"I won't repeat myself, Beta. Stand down." With a harsh shove, he releases his hold and then hops up, standing above the warlock with a glare. And yet no one mentions the stench coming down off him. "Take him to the cells for questioning. Be as accommodating as you please."

"Yes, Alpha." Two guards step forward, each taking an arm. The warlock is forced to his feet, shoved, and dragged back onto our lands, but before crossing the entrance, his eyes meet mine over his shoulder.

There's a challenge there. The stink of rubbish and spoilage is also stomach-turning.

"Long live my queen, your majesty."

7
Isabella

I'm running.

Shivering and with my heart pounding, I push myself harder while stillness overtakes the forest. My footfalls are loud in the silence while soft, gasping breaths escape my chest, burning as adrenaline builds and my core tightens from excitement.

Tonight, I am his prey.

Afraid and thrilled while the yearning I've had no choice but to bury down deep overtakes me. I embrace it, though, this crazy game we're playing. Having his attention focused solely on me is addictive, and the beading of my nipples through the thin white dress I'm wearing is a sign of that. So is the flush of my cheeks and goose bumps on my skin.

However, it's the wetness between my thighs the animal wants.

His warning growls make me whimper. Loud and thundering, it cracks, and the sound echoes throughout the landscape. Each one settles deep within my DNA, a private calling for his mate, and I almost drop to my knees.

Instead, I stumble, blindly reaching a hand out to the nearest trunk, using it to brace my weakening form. That low vibration ripples across every nerve ending, and I want to submit. To rip my clothes off and present my body, make myself available to his every desire.

Because pleasing him is all I want to do.

Xadiel Evergreen will be my first and last. No other man will ever touch me.

Today. Tomorrow. Always.

My vow is bonding. Carved into our existence.

"Gods help me." The soothing scent of cedar and mint envelops me, becoming stronger the longer I stay against this trunk, and I push off again. The bottom of my dress drags over the ground, becoming filthy as it snags on a low branch, and I almost bend down to rip off the torn hem.

Almost. Because no sooner do I reach down to lift it, my bare feet still rushing through the moonlit forest, I feel the tips of claws graze my arm. That's all he does. Just a touch, but it's enough to pull a wanton moan from me.

Deprivation does that to a person. My need for him is magnified and painful.

Tilting my head slightly, I keep my eyes on where I'd been. I'm walking backward now, glancing between the foliage but his massive form evades me. Blends into the night, yet right as I turn to run, his voice stops me.

"You're a bad girl, Little Moon. So mischievous." Gravelly, his tone is dark and rich. There's also a small tinge of anger underneath, *exasperation at his own uncontrolled desire.* "You haunt me, Isabella. Every moment of every day. Even in my dreams."

"You chose this. Not me."

"I did." *He's also closer. Toying with me.* "But you know the why."

"Lies." *That's what keeps us apart.* "You chose to believe—"

A large shadow moves from the left, the swiftness making me flinch, and I lose my footing on a thick root. Not that I ever fall. He's there in an instant, his black-tipped claws gripping my dress and keeping me upright. The fabric tears, the sound reverberating around us while those eyes, golden with black swirls, stay on mine.

So much emotion in them. So much regret.

"How are you so fast?" *Something akin to a snort comes from him before releasing me. Xadiel doesn't answer. Instead, he tilts his head to the side in an appraising move. From head to toe, the sinful stare is a caress, and I take a step back out of instinct.*

Just one. Then another.

I need the space to think and catch my breath, but my mate doesn't like it.

His lip curls over razor-sharp canines. "Don't move."

"Or what?" *I'm taunting him. A behavior so out of character for me. Of the two sisters, I've always been the calmer one. Less sassy.* "You don't want me, remember?"

Another retreating movement. More space between us, and yet I'm aware of the looming trees at my back, a few monstrous sequoias I didn't notice my last time here; the largest of the trio is close enough that if I reach behind me, I'd touch the bark.

"Final warning, my witch." *I won't deny that my entire body comes alive at the term of endearment. That wetness slips from where I'm throbbing and needy, something the sudden flaring of his nose and low grunt of approval tells me he's aware of.* "You know I do. That's never been the problem, Isabella."

"Then what...oh fuck!" *His hand is around my throat before my next blink, tight and strong, lifting me off the ground and then*

51

pinning me with his body, pressing his thickness between my thighs. Thighs that part and with the nudge of his other hand, they wrap around his waist. My dress has ridden up, exposing my legs and the edge of my mound, but if he were to lean back, I have no doubt Xadiel would see it all: weakness, wetness, and my inability to say no to him.

The bark of the tree digs into my back, but the slight sting of pain only enhances my arousal. So does the pricks on my skin where the tips of his fangs now slide against my mouth; I couldn't stop myself from shifting just enough to feel them.

Want more, though. My body screams for it.

"Denying you hurts more than you could possibly imagine." His wolf is present. Growly and garbled, those words are his. He hurts, too. "Why can't I stop myself from wanting you? Why is hating you such an uphill battle?"

Not that I'm given much time to ponder this because immediately after, his lips are on mine.

Dominant and all-consuming, Xadiel kisses me with the perfect combination of the two. He steals my first kiss like he did my heart, without remorse while those clawed fingers move from my neck to the back of my skull, pulling the red strands.

The sharp tug stings and my lips part, something he takes advantage of. Warm and soft, his tongue slips against my own and the sensation is addictive. So is his taste; purely him and seductive.

Tilting my head back to his liking, Xadiel purrs into my mouth. It vibrates through me from head to toe and then settles on my clit. The feeling is indescribable. So good.

"More. Please."

That earns me a chuckle and a roll of his trouser-covered hips, sharp teeth digging into my bottom lip. Then he drags them back, piercing the flesh. Small and stinging, the cut bleeds and he laps at it —groans while gifting me another quick thrust, his thickness jerking right where I want him most.

I'm near tears. Delirious with yearning. Yet Xadiel pulls back, his hold still tight with those beautiful eyes on me. Gold with a deep onyx swirl. "You're the sweetest treat, Little Moon. A surprise I need."

"Then stop holding back."

"I can't." Two words, and they hit me in the gut. As if punched.

"Please let me open your eyes." Meek. My plea is honest and full of hurt.

"I'm sorry. Truly am." Xadiel releases me then, making sure I'm steady before stepping back. The separation is like a lash across my skin. Breaks me. Bleeds me. "This is all I can give you."

Swallowing back my emotions, I stand straight. My eyes shine with unshed tears, but they don't fall. I refuse to let them. "We will meet three times, Xadiel Evergreen. Twice you've disappointed me— after the last, there will be no going back."

"Isa—"

*"I'll remove you from my flesh. **I iurare**."*

I awake with a start the second that vow leaves my lips, my thigh throbbing—burning—stealing the very breath from my lungs just like it did a year ago. The first time I dreamed of him, my wolf. Yet today, the pain is just as blinding and I want to scream, but instead bite down on my bottom lip and pray to the gods that it ends.

I try to push the memory of our first kiss from my thoughts. It might not have been in person, but in the dream world, I was his. Felt his skin, the sharpness of his desire, and those lips on mine.

Panting breaths escape me and I lick my dry lips, still finding a trace of Xadiel on them.

A painful reminder. A glorious gift.

Having the ability to walk through dreams is something our mother taught us when we were young, to meet a loved one in the realm of slumber, an insurance in case we were ever taken or hurt. It doesn't work with everyone; a strong bond or emotion must tie you together, and mine with the werewolf king wraps around me like a vice grip.

But today, it brought me to heaven and then slammed me straight back to hell.

Unyielding. Unbreakable. Unforgiving. *For now.*

A reality that furthers my misery.

"How will I forgive him?" I whisper to my empty bedroom back home. We arrived back on our familial sacred ground after days of traveling—a time where truths my sister had no choice but to confront slapped her in the face. They hurt me too. To know our people, those we trusted, were the cause of so much pain.

So many witches dead. So many more hurt.

That dungeon where we found the women and children, all abused and incarcerated for their blood, was a nightmare. Heartbreaking to find them so afraid—malnourished and mistreated by their coven leader who for years faked his love for my family. Salicio's loyalty was easily broken by the promise of money and power.

"How can I leave the ones who need me here?" I won't deny that it's an option. And while the universe has a way of always placing us where we need to be, I want to deny destiny the pleasure of my tears.

A gentle breeze sweeps into the room from the open window, and I throw my legs over the edge of the bed while ignoring the pain. It's settled a bit, more a low throb now, and the cool floor feels good on my feet.

As if pulled by a string, I walk over to the window and gaze up at the sky. The moon is high tonight, full and beautiful while illuminating the area where my ever-present tormentor marks me as his.

Large and bold, the perfect image of his dark wolf, the piece encompasses the entire expanse of my thigh—beautiful and intricate —a mirror image of his beast. I also won't deny it's given me solace through lonely nights when I have missed him, but tonight it's the opposite.

I'm torn. Struggling.

Duty or love. My people or my pride.

Going back to England will cost me. Of that, there's no doubt. *But how much? What will be left of me?*

We met by the lake and in our dreams, but each time I'm the one who walks away. There's no other choice. My heart evades the possibility of hearing the words that will forever break our bond. Even now, my breathing becomes choppy at the mere thought, and the muscle inside my chest squeezes tight.

The tattoo also strikes again with an acid-like blaze that rips a scream from my throat and I bite down on my knuckle, breaking the dermis. Blood stains my mouth and my skin is on fire, but it's the unspoken words that haunt me.

I, Xadiel Evergreen, reject Isabella Moore, as my mate and Luna.

Is that my future the next time we meet?

"Get it together, Isabella. You are stronger than this." Then again, it's being here again. Surrounded by memories. Their scent that lingers in every nook and cranny of our childhood home. Mom and Dad are everywhere, and I've been so focused on my siblings, setting them on the right path, that I've neglected my emotions.

So, I let the tears fall.

One after another, I sob for our parents and how much I miss them. I cry for the man who was meant to be mine but wishes my kind dead over someone's greed and lies.

I let out everything I've bottled inside for the sake of not worrying my siblings while the moon sits high, watching. It bathes me in its light while the breeze wraps me in a hug that carries the lavish scent of lavender and reminds me of...

"Mom." The winds pick up a bit, whipping at my face, and I close my eyes. I can almost feel her wiping each cheek, can almost hear her telling me everything will be okay, but just as soon, it dies down.

I'm on my own again.

I also have a promise to keep.

"The path to happiness is paved by tears."

"I've been looking for you, Isabella. Are you okay?" Meera asks, finding me inside my father's office with a stack of papers in my hand. We're following through on his final request, my sister and me, emptying the rooms of anything belonging to him and the family estate, from every document and book to familial heirlooms passed down from generation to generation.

Jewelry meant only for the Wiccan king and queen.

All of it will go into private storage for now; secret rooms that are only accessible by our command and hidden behind stone doors. There are three of those vaults on the estate and at various points. Moreover, without Gabriella and me, there is no access. No one knows the spell, and Leo is too young for that kind of responsibility.

I want the house ready for his return. To be as back to normal as can be.

"I'm fine, Meera." Emptying the last drawer in his desk, I gather the land ownership title and place it with other important papers. They'll be locked inside weatherproofed metal boxes. "Just a little tired."

"I can see that."

That stops me and I look up, raising a brow. "Definitely need a bath, but I'm not *that* bad. It's just a bit dusty in here and—"

"You're carrying the weight of the world on those shoulders." Meera's eyes have seen so much—she survived her father's wickedness. The betrayal and abuse. But right now, her worry is for me; she sees what I've kept hidden for so long. "Who do *you* lean on, my princess? Who helps with those burdens?"

"Promise, Meera. I'm okay."

"You're not, but I'm not going to push you." She shrugs, smile small. "Just know I'm here if you ever need me. After everything you've done for me and my—" Meera chokes up, and I'm around the desk and wrapping my hands around her fragile frame in seconds.

Two days ago, she'd been alone in a darkened cell and chained to the ground. Thin, dirty, and bled for the dark magic her coven wielded.

She's strong, though. Salicio didn't break her spirit.

I've also seen that she'll meet her mate soon. He resides with the vampires and will treat her like a queen, even if their start will be rocky.

I don't tell her this. Instead, I hug her close, mindful of her bruises. Then I give her a bit of my strength, the same way I've done with my sister in the past. Witches can do this with someone they care about, and I feel the change in her almost immediately.

Her posture straightens and legs no longer shake. "Someday you're going to have to let someone be there for you, Isa. Giving is both good and admirable, but accepting is just as humbling."

"I will. One day."

"Good."

"What's good?" Gabriella asks, stepping into the room. She's freshened up since I last saw her hours ago while she tended to the master bedroom and the removal of everything important or sentimental in there. Those were placed in another hidden depository. "Did something happen?"

"No, but what's with the satchel and candles? Are we—"

"We need to be with them. Who knows when we'll be back."

"Are you sure?" From the corner of my eye, I catch Meera slipping from the room. She closes the door behind her to give us privacy. *Bruises and memories fade with time; her shifter will make it so. He will make her so happy, and they both will be there for Gabby when the time comes.*

"Yes, Sister. Especially if we're leaving tonight."

8
ALPHA XADIEL

I can still taste her on my lips.

So sweet and decadent.

It's all I've been able to think about since waking from the erotic dream more than a week ago; the heady pleasure of having her against me, in my arms, and then the feeling of dread soon after waking with a hard cock and sweat glistening on my skin. She wasn't there beside me. No mate to love, cherish, or sink into.

This is the second time; a warning Isabella Moore gave me and I believe it—her—that the moment we shared was real. Of that, there's no doubt in my mind. We played a game of hunter and prey; I wanted to mount and mark. Seal our bond with my bite.

Even if I regretted it after.

Even if it hurt us and tore our lives apart until the day we reunite again. Late in this lifetime or the next. Or maybe once we reach our final resting place where wolves and their mates find eternal solace. There, I could give her what physically and emotionally, fate stole.

How the visit came to be? No clue, but I won't deny I'm grateful for the gift.

"Please let me open your eyes."

A plea I ignored, knowing that words won't change our reality. However, the finality in her parting promise struck a chord deep within my soul and made me doubt for the briefest of seconds.

Heavy and honest, she warned me.

*"I'll remove you from my flesh. **I iurare.**"*

The last two words I didn't understand. Not then. However, witches aren't the only species with books on other languages. Old and hard to find, I procured a Latin dictionary in our library, the section on our origin story, and found the two words under another vow.

Because that's what my little moon did. Promised to forget me. Rip me from her very essence.

"Over my dead body," I snarl, pushing away a paper I'd been reading. Pack business, a request to visit a family member in the Spaniard territories that needs my signature, yet I can't focus enough on it to sign. Because that's the one thing the wolf and I agree on: she's not rejecting or replacing us.

Hypocritical of me, I know, but don't give a fuck either way.

I might've walked away and refused to accept her, but I never spoke the words. The bond is there, thriving and strong, and it's staying that way.

My fangs drop, and a heavy rumble builds in the back of my throat that quickly turns into a growl—angry and determined—at the mere thought. Wanting her has never been the issue. My mate is simply stunning, the scent of jasmines my personal nirvana, but there's something I just can't see past.

It'd be a slap in the faces of my family and pack. My mum is dead because of hers.

From one extreme to another, I want and I hate, then back again. A never-ending punishment. I've thought through this and tried to make sense of all angles, but the question remains: could we move past this?

Would she forgive me after I crushed her parents hearts with my bare hands?

My wolf whines at the implication of hurting Isabella, the noise full of so much sadness and I rub my chest, trying to soothe the beast. He doesn't see the world as I do, and nothing comes before one's mate. Yet I can't do the same.

Rejecting her is right, but at what cost?

My wolf's sanity. My humanity.

"I can't live with her, but I can't let her go either." Exhaling, I sit back in my chair and close my eyes. At once, it's her face I see. The big blue doe eyes and supple mouth, the soft curl at the upper right of her lips, and then the way she bit them when I held her throat. How her chest rose and fell quickly. How she mewled for me, shaking under my grip while her dress slid up and exposed the red strip of her hair just above her clit.

Neat, and the same shade as on her head—each hair artfully removed.

Soft while just the tiniest bit of wetness clung to the well-trimmed curls, the rest of her is bare.

I swallow hard. Wishing I'd taken a taste against the large tree.

Hating her for the temptation.

Hating myself for wanting to forget my reasons and run after her. Claim what's mine.

"We need to talk, Xadiel." Gamma Cain says, entering my office, pulling me from my thoughts, and my lids snap open. He shuts the door behind him before turning to face me, his expression one of stubborn determination. It immediately deflates my cock and I push those lingering thoughts—my wants—out of my head for now.

He's one of the few here I'd let address me without the title. Something my best friend doesn't take advantage of.

"Everything okay?" I ask, waving him forward to take a seat.

Cain takes the one across from me, watching me carefully. His head tilts. "You tell me. There's something you're not sharing?"

"What's that supposed to mean?" My brows furrow and my jaw ticks. Lately, my fuse is a little shorter. Moods fluctuate constantly, and it's all her fault. My eternal torment.

"You've been acting *strange*, Xadiel."

"Have I?" Didn't think anyone would notice.

"Yes." A bit more relaxed, my gamma crosses an ankle over the knee, then drums his fingers against the armrest. He's also smiling; whatever he sees on my face amuses him. "Cranky, secretive, and lost in thought. Everyone's been avoiding you in case you snap, but I recognize the pattern. Had something similar happen to me in the few days between finding my mate and her moving here."

"You're wrong, Cain. I didn't—"

"And you're a shit liar. Try that with someone who doesn't know you."

Running a tired hand down my face, I tug at the small beard growing on my chin. A new addition over the last few weeks. "It's complicated."

"Then uncomplicate it." His exasperation almost makes me smile. *If only he knew.* "This is our luna and queen you're talking about, Xadiel. Her place is here. With her people."

"A *witch* has no place in my kingdom. She never will." That stops him short while guilt settles deep in my gut. I'd spat the word with so much venom and hate; for her mother and kind and the possibility Isabella could've been involved. Even though my heart tells me this is unfair, my wolf scratches against my skin, his claws tearing me from within at the pain I'm causing, yet my feelings are just.

The truth. Our fate.

"Brother, don't pin your ire on an innocent girl. She's not at fault for—"

"Isabella Moore is my mate, Cain. That's what I'm fighting against."

"Well, shit, Alpha." I'm thankful he keeps his face blank of emotions this time. Pity is the last thing I want to see. From him or anyone.

"Exactly."

For a while, neither of us speaks. We're deep in thought, and the room feels heavy and volatile, too. The latter is all me. Disappointment leads to anger on its way to a yearning so cruel I close my fist and allow my claws to pierce through my flesh, feeling the droplets of blood as they pool and then fall onto my trousers where I'm keeping them out of sight.

"Do you believe in the moon goddess and her purpose? Trust her?" Cain asks, breaking the silence. It's also not where I thought he'd go, but I nod in response. Our goddess has never failed her children, but this isn't her hand at play. This wickedness comes from the witches and their greed.

"Would she pair you with someone cruel and evil?"

"My heart says no, but the reality is different."

"Or so you think." Standing, Cain taps my desk with his closed fist before doing the same to his chest. A sign of solidarity. "Sometimes the sweetest reward starts as the cruelest of tasks. Remember that, Xadiel. There's a reason for everything."

"Cain, I—"

Alpha, we've finished setting up as you requested.

A smirk spreads across my face at that. This is how I'll get my answers.

"Why do you have that look? Is she here?"

"No." Pushing my chair back, I stand and crack my neck. The loud sound reverberates around the room. "But I am going to enjoy myself."

"I'm not following, Xadiel."

"I have a date with a warlock and two miserable arsehole guards." Understanding dawns, and Cain smiles too, just as sinister and dark. "Join me in the dungeons in about two hours. I'm going to need your assistance with something."

"Yes, Alpha. I'm just going to run a quick perimeter check before then." His reply, while compliant, isn't honest. He'll be back to ask questions and prod, not letting go like a dog with a bone, but I'm glad for the chance to leave it for now.

"Good. Because it's time to play."

SINCE CAPTURING THE WARLOCK, I'D YET TO VISIT HIM. INSTEAD, I've let him stew in his filth for days on end—that acrid stench of decay that clings to his flesh but no one else can sense.

I do, though, and his death is near. It permeates the air, on the clothes of those who monitor him, and I'm enjoying it. His misery makes me smile.

His refusal to eat or talk only makes this sweeter.

Because by my hand or fate, the arsehole will suffer. Nothing will change that.

Not when every tick of the clock is a tightening noose forecasting his demise. How his life slowly fades, his powers subdued, and those charged with monitoring him report back daily with every minute detail.

He's bound every second of the day with his hands splayed open and an opal-stoned dagger embedded in each, which he cannot remove. The blade is encrusted in the wall of his cell, a containment unit blessed and warded by the same woman whose head I want to be crushed beneath my boot.

Irony: what a beautiful cunt she is. The bloody queen helping me without knowing.

And even while chained to a wall, at my mercy, he's been volatile and angry. Threatening those around him...*until* earlier today.

He's unable to lift his head. The bastard refuses to while playing an immobile corpse, yet the moment I step inside the cell, his head snaps up and his body begins to shake, thrashing so hard his palms are cut straight down from the center to the wrist and out through the side, just shy of the veins there.

However, the sharp blade remains intact and in place.

Blood seeps from the wound, but it's not the fresh sanguine drops one would expect. No. This is darker, thicker too, almost coagulated in its consistency. The descent is slow, and I watch as a drop at a time becomes puddles beneath his feet.

The robe he's wearing does little to hide how emaciated he's become in just a few days.

Pallid, dirty, and greasy. But awareness is clear in his stare. "You know."

Not a question, but I nod yet the same. Whatever is killing him is causing this. "I do."

"For how long? How?"

Ignoring him, I walk deeper into the room. In the corner, there's a stack of stale bread and a large jug of water. The guards left a tray with other weapons on the opposite side; all are clean and unused— all but the blade of a golden dagger that catches my eye.

Taking the few steps between myself and the knife, I bend and pick it up. It's thick and heavy, the sharp edge glinting in the low lighting coming off the singular torch.

My fingers wrap around the hilt. "Bring me his meal."

"Answer me, *Alpha*. How do you know?"

"Now," I say, ignoring his emphasis on my title. From the corner of my eye, I catch the two guards exchanging a look. Neither questions me, though. Grady has always been loyal, and his son, a trainee, is showing great character. "It should be right outside the door by now."

"Yes, Alpha." The younger of the two rushes out, bringing with him a domed-lid plate and a still-hot cuppa. "Where do you want me to put this, King Xadiel?"

At once, the scent of a full English breakfast fills the stone room with iron bars. I've spared no expense for my guests, plural, and one of them will enjoy a bountiful last meal.

Every act of madness has a purpose.

The smallest temptations can move mountains.

"Hold them for a moment." I bite back a smirk while the warlock's fear intensifies. So does an unmistakable rumble from his abdomen. Because there are many ways to break a person: witches, fae, vampires, and werewolves all share one likeness to humans we can't control. We feel…

Hunger.

Desperation.

Pain.

"Better yet, let's all take a walk. Some fresh air would do him good."

9
ALPHA
XADIEL

"I'm not eating that."

"What is *that*...?" I raise a brow. "Afraid I'd poison you?"

"How about you answer some questions, your highness? Tell me how you know," he sneers, a lot more alert now than when I arrived, but it's false valor. The piss pooling, mixing with his bloodstains on the concrete floor, is a good tell. So is the way he flinches when I toss the knife, catching it with my now-clawed hand.

My wolf has risen to the surface. The animal is in my eyes and the sudden sprout of fur covering my arms and chest. It's bothersome, the bulging of my muscles ripping the back of my long-sleeved shirt, and I toss it.

I don't care where it lands. Instead, I take in how uncomfortable this man is.

"You know the answer to that already. Don't you." Not a question, and the way he shifts his eyes away confirms it. Turning, I look at Grady. "Bring him to the lowest floor. We're already late for a meeting."

Exiting the room, I take a walk down the opposite end of the floor and find the two cells empty, their occupants having been moved, and I step inside the first. Just like the warlock's, this one has a stack of old bread, a jug of water, and chains on the wall. The difference here is the silver used to keep the wolf subdued; it doesn't kill the beast but will slow him down.

Unless injected. In the bloodstream, it's toxic.

However, there's something different here. The fresh scent of a kill. Meat.

Moving deeper into the room, I kick aside the food and find nothing. On the left, there's a tattered blanket, unapproved by me, and I find nothing beneath it. Yet I smell it. The animal within me does, too.

Closing my eyes, I center myself before inhaling deeply again. This time, the note of deer is sharper and my feet move at once. They lead me to a wall and my lids snap open, taking in the sole window —a small square large enough to fit a human head and nothing else.

Yet, there's a dry red residue on the edge.

Old and yet new. As if delivered a few hours prior to my arrival in the prison.

Stupidity has a name.

The two captured and kept alive have no mates. No offspring. They're nothing more than a means to an end, my connection to those responsible, and I've been patient. More so than I should've been, but fools never learn.

Never underestimate my tolerance for stupidity.

Everyone has a weakness.

This prisoner's vulnerability is a woman. Young and impressionable and who has pled with me on her brother's behalf for as long as he's resided here.

The next room is much the same. Only no extra meals.

Suddenly, the sound of struggling catches my attention. There are screams of obscenities, threats are made, and I smirk.

"Let the games begin."

FOR AN HOUR, I LET THEM SIT.

Each arsehole is strapped to a chair, his chains tight and the sight of fresh injuries blatant to the eye. Just like the lack of healing from all three, especially the male witch. His old and new wounds are infected: red and angry with hints of a mucus-like substance around the edges.

Interesting to say the least.

However, all attention is on me. Bloodshot eyes follow my every move while lips form words but no sounds come out, the sight of my animal dragging the carcass of a fresh kill causing hearts to beat fast. For breathing to become choppy while the sweet taste of my solo hunt lingers on my tongue.

I've had my fill.

My prey's life essence drips from the two canines bared at the trio while an irate snarl rips from deep within my chest. Moreover, it's comical when the heavy iron doors keeping us locked inside slam shut a second later and they jump.

Right now, it's just us. No other guard or anyone to stop me from what must be done.

We're enclosed, a place so deep underground that their screams will never be heard.

The time of hospitality is over. I want answers.

Taking the steps between us, I pass by the three men. Slowly.

Growling. Each body stills, trying to not react to the snapping of my teeth, but that only serves to amuse me.

Their fear is a heady concoction. Delicious.

Coming to a stop in front of the small dining table between us now, I regain control and shift. My anatomy resyncs—bones and muscles realign with the human construction while the animal falls back. The wolf's features re-form into a sharp jaw with a short beard while the fangs stay.

"Who's hungry?" I ask, but there's no verbal response. Don't expect one, either. Instead, one man's hunger rises, and the gleam of black is a sign of his animal attempting to take over. He tries to shift and struggles against his binds while the other guard remains calm.

He wants the kill, but the earlier meal keeps him from lunging forward like his friend.

Starved. Going to die. In Cecil's weakness, the mental link opens and I'm able to hear every thought. So does his friend and partner-in-crime, Jack, who's shaking in his seat, but the other is too far gone to understand. His animal needs to be fed and demands he grab the kill, but those silver chains keep him from moving. They dig into his skin, burning him, yet his mind is too far gone. *Bartolo lied. Everyone lied.*

"What about you, Jack?" A pair of trousers lies over a chair in the corner, the golden knife I picked up earlier inside the pocket. They watch me get dressed. Jump at any sudden movement. "There's more than enough for the both of you."

"I'm sorry, Alpha—"

"Keep your empty apologies and answer the question. Are you starving?"

Both werewolves have lost some body mass, yet Jack is less gauntly. "Yes. I am."

"Liar."

"Your majesty, I—"

"Insulting my intelligence isn't in your best interest, arsehole.

Don't lie to me." Placing my palm face down on the table, I lean forward. "Did you really think I wouldn't know?"

He swallows hard at the underlying threat. "She's a pup, Alpha. Just a kid worried about her brother who made a huge mistake and is paying for it. I'll talk to her—"

"I'm not cruel to those who don't deserve it, Jack."

"Please don't hurt her."

"I won't..." keeping my expression neutral, I drag my nails down the wood "...but I don't do it for you."

He exhales roughly, shoulders losing their rigidity. "Thank you for the mercy, my king."

"You've brought shame and heartache to your family, Jack." His face pinches tight at the reproach, as if in immense pain, and his scent has changed, too. Reeks of desperation; not sure if it's to get away from me or gain my forgiveness. Neither matter, nor will it change his sentencing. "Your selfishness has put your younger sister in a difficult position, and I'll forgive *her* because I understand. You do anything for those you love."

"I'll forever be in your debt."

"How pathetic," the male witch sneers.

"Please enlighten me." A smile tugs at my lips as my eyes cut toward the warlock. His stench is deeper, a stomach-turning scent of burnt rubbish that the others are oblivious to. From his dirty form to the untouched breakfast, I take him in. Just like this. "Oh, wise one."

"You're overconfident now, but my true ruler will make you pay. Everything you love, he will take from you."

"Is that so, Bartolo?" Surprise flashes across his face, a quick shock, but then he schools his features. The man has no idea how attuned I am to his moves and changes, the sickness running through his veins and killing him one breath at a time.

Yet, he'll never make it that far. I'll end his life before his time is up.

I also didn't miss his slip. Bartolo said *he,* not her.

Paolo is not just protecting his wife but also the puppet master. Both are cruel and traitors.

Does Isabella know? Has she been a part of this betrayal?

Before his next labored breath, the cup of tea in front of him is smashed into the side of his head. It whips to the left, the object shattering upon impact, and I embed a sharp porcelain piece into his temple and then force the jagged piece down to his cheek. The wound opens—skin splitting under the pressure—and darkened blood rolls down the side until reaching his jaw.

Drop after drop; I watch each one with a morbid fascination. Is this how all witches bleed?

To his credit, the warlock doesn't cry out. His scent intensifies, but not a sound.

Is my little moon as wicked?

A question that pisses me the fuck off. Anger rolls through my veins and I crack my neck, ready to rip his throat out, but then another thought comes to mind. His fear intensified the moment he realized I sensed death all around him.

Something about that knowledge throws him off.

Does he know who my mate is? Is she the reason why I sense his unease?

I'm going to enjoy this.

"Tell me, Jack. What did they promise you to betray us?" Pulling the blade from my pocket, I flip it open and examine the blade. It's a beautiful piece, shiny and sharp, and so smooth when piercing the human skin we walk around in. Jack's scream attests to that. "Answer me."

"Money, and a new position in the pack after they took over." This comes out on a whimper; one his friend mimics. Cecil is lost to his animal. Moved by self-preservation and hunger, his claws still reaching for the meat just a few feet away. "All they asked us to do was take a break at a certain time. That's all."

"That's all?" As if they didn't help kill an innocent woman.

"Yes, my king."

"Who contacted you?" I hiss out through clenching teeth, reaching for the hilt and pulling out the knife in one quick tug. "Names, Jack. All of them."

No sooner has the last word slipped through my lips than Jack and Cecil begin to thrash. They're foaming at the mouth, eyes pure black now and their expressions showing torture.

I let it happen.

Let them feel the sting of Bartolo's power with a bored expression on my face.

Taking a seat, I relax back and watch. Wait.

And the longer he manipulates them, the weaker he becomes. The more their cries grow in volume; I find myself enjoying the horror-filled sound.

Justice comes in many forms, and this is one of them.

Bartolo doesn't stop, and soon enough both men pass out from the pain. His magic is dark, an aura that surrounds him—I can make out each individual tendril as it strikes the wolves strapped to a chair like a whip. Small cuts appear across their chest and arms, small rivulets of bright red flow from each one, and still, I don't intervene.

This is the price of betrayal. The beginning.

As much as it hurts my heart to hurt one of my own, I can't forgive. Won't.

Cecil and Jack will serve two years of torture inside separate cells. Each day, a new serving of fresh meat will be placed within their room while they're chained, the silver preventing them from shifting, and they'll wither away slowly. They'll be kept barely alive by bread and water until they're released and then banished from the pack.

I should kill them, but the plea of their kin saved them. This is the only mercy I can show.

A quick flick of my wrist and the bloodied knife is in the warlock's shoulder. Deep. "Motherfuck," he cries out, and the enchantment breaks. Now what comes out of his mouth is a loud wail, expletives, and the screeching of his chair against the floor as he tries to move.

Stand. Fight. Pull the blade out but the chain keeps him in place. So, I help him.

Standing from my seat, I make my way around and release one damaged hand. "Eat."

"You're going to pay for this. Lose everyone you love."

"You mean like my mate?" He grows pallid, and it's not from injuries or blood loss. This is more. Different. "Enlighten me, Bartolo. Why did it take you a year to return? Why are you here?"

"I might've waited too long. Plans had to be set in motion, but she is a risk."

"A risk for me or you? Those pulling your strings?"

"You'll never know. I vow it."

"Sure about that?"

"Tell me this..." Bartolo tries to right himself and grimaces, eyeing the blade and then me "...did you know that the Moore family owns land not far from here? That all this time, you could've found me. Killed my queen, but didn't." My wolf rises at the challenge, the taunt, and my claws rip through my nail beds. Muscles bulging and chest rising with deep breaths, I don't answer but keep my glare on the sallow man. "The Wiccan royals are corrupt, King Evergreen. If anyone should fear Isabella, it's you. She's going to—"

He doesn't get to finish.

I react, and within seconds his face is smashed into the English breakfast plate. Once, twice...five times; I slam his head into the mess and table, breaking more than the porcelain. A split in the wood appears and the mess spreads, mixing with the dark life's essence dripping from his wounds.

Bartolo's eyes roll back and his front teeth crack, breaking and cutting his lips.

My nails dig into his scalp, tearing through the skin, but Cain's voice through the mind link stops me.

Xadiel, we have a situation.

Tightening my grip, I rip a section of his scalp off. Toss it by his cheek. *What?*

Your mate is here.

Coincidence, or planned? Either way, I'll get the answers to the questions plaguing my mind.

We can't be together, but I won't deny the flare of excitement at seeing her. Touching her again.

And while I can't kill Isabella, physically hurt her, if she's involved in any way...

I'll break her.

Reject her even if it's my demise, as well. We'll destroy each other.

Escort her to my office. No one touches her.

Leaning down, I place my mouth next to his ear and chuckle. "Your princess is here. She came to see me." Bartolo tries to whisper an incantation through split lips, the scent of his desperation rising. The reaper clings to him a little harder, yet I stop him by sinking the black-tipped claws of my other hand into his back. "Try that again, and death will never have the chance to claim you. I see it. Can smell it on you, arsehole."

"Fuck you."

"I'm going to enjoy ripping your throat out when the time comes." Pulling my nails out, I pat the torn flesh. "Now, we have a meeting with my mate, and I dare you to disappoint her."

10

Isabella

L eaving everyone behind was hard but the right thing to do. More so because my people need protection.

Danger is coming. Its looming presence is palpable; I feel it and Gabriella does too.

She told me as much before leaving to find her vampire. The threat from within isn't over. There are witches working to end our bloodline—who want the crown—and are willing to kill every Moore descendant for it.

It doesn't matter that Leo is a child. That Gabriella and I are whom they should fear.

Greed and power doesn't see reasoning or accept common sense. These people are blind to it.

The one who attempts to block my powers is sloppy at times. This hold is tentative and wavers, glimpses of what's to come still filter through. Then, there are moments where the blinders come off and it's clear, as if I'm sitting amid the chaos they created.

"The end is coming," I whisper under my breath, breathing in deep, the soothing salt air surrounding me. The early morning hours are accompanied by a semi-thick layer of fog, fresh and foreboding, but I'm not afraid. If anything, I find calm in the heavy mist and let it soothe my tired muscles.

I've traveled for days. From Italy to France, riding our Salernitano horses through our beloved forest until reaching the Parisian border. The breed is strong and are enchanted to withstand the rough ride, yet the ones we own are special. Pearl was my mother's, while Onyx belonged to Father.

I have one and Gabby has the other.

The rest are offspring of the two and are being used by our guards back home, each named after the solstice they were born under.

Like the last time we left our lands, we could've teleported if we wished to, but that would leave a heavy trace of our powers for days on end, something the most novice witch could detect and follow. Risking it would've been foolish, just like opening one directly to Xadiel's land could be my demise. At the moment, I'm an enemy.

And if my siblings and I are killed or taken as slaves, then who would protect our kind from what's to come? No one. We're all they have now.

And while the route this time is different, I didn't stop until reaching King Larue's land. There, I took pause and reached for the small pouch I'd hidden within the horse's saddle. Small and brimming with shimmery powder, I poured the contents on the grassy ground, creating a circle a few feet from where we stood. At once, the ground gave a subtle shake and a headache formed at the back of my skull, one that would pass in a minute or two.

The tremble, however, was more pronounced—felt—where a tall oval appeared.

Like a two-way mirror, I could see the huge boat awaiting us on the other side. People roamed, walking in front of the doorway, completely oblivious. It stayed that way for a few minutes after we crossed, giving us safe passage and time to stow the horses below.

That was hours ago, and now the British port is on the horizon. Far away, yet close enough that the sounds of men yelling and a loud foghorn greets my ears. This is a land I've visited a few times, beautiful and serene, but more importantly, it's home now.

Maybe always has been. The kinship to this country has always been there, growing and pulling me, but it didn't make sense until *him*. My Xadiel.

I was always meant to end up here.

But for how long?

He could always choose to reject me. A truth that hurts, and I rub the skin where my beating heart lies underneath. Throbbing, the organ gives another painful squeeze and I almost lose my footing. Yet before I face plant or worse, go over the rail, Augusto's there. His hand grips my arm, pulling back and holding me steady while I catch my breath.

My mother's personal guard has always been loyal to the crown and our family. He's one of the few people I trust blindly; I've also never been happier to have someone follow me.

He made the trip easier. Didn't let me drown in my thoughts.

"Are you okay, Princess?"

"I am." Taking in a deep breath, I let it out slowly. My hands on the rail grip tight enough to turn my knuckles white. "This trip should set me free. Break or heal me, but at least I'll know…you know?"

"I do."

My eyes shift his way. "That sounds ominous."

"My mate hated me when we first met." Not at all what I expected him to say, and my expression shows it. That makes him laugh, the sound loud and boisterous, catching the attention of other people close by. "I'm serious. Ileana hated my guts and thought I was a weird man. Her words, not mine."

"Weird?"

"I might've had a staring problem the night we met."

I can't help but giggle at the sheepish look he gives me and the pink coloring his cheeks. "Please do tell."

His wife is a beautiful witch who makes the best pastries. She's our dealer—everyone knows the Moore sisters have a sweet tooth—and I can't picture her disliking him. Just can't. They're almost sugary together, always smiling and giving innocent touches when in the other's presence.

"As corny as this may sound, that woman bewitched me." The grin on his face is wide, from ear to ear, and affection pours out of him. It's heartwarming and open, his emotions calming the tumultuous nerves that are rising the closer we get to shore.

In less than half a day's travel, I'll be on his property.

Face to face once again.

"I'm going to tell her you said that."

"But it's the Gods' truth." Augusto chuckles, as if remembering that day. "One look and my soul recognized her as mine; I couldn't be without her. Not that she didn't feel the same, even if she swears it took her days to accept me. I claimed my bride that same night and twined our lives for the rest of time."

"That's beautiful." A lone tear falls, and I'm quick to wipe it away while he stares out at the bustling city port. "True love is a gift, Augusto. May the Gods bless you both."

"Thank you, Princess." For a few beats we're silent, but then he nods to himself. "I know I'm not your father or a family member, but you three mean the world to me and Ileana."

"We care deeply for you, too."

Augusto's head tilts toward me, expression soft and eyes holding nothing but sincerity. Warmth. "You three are the future of all witches, Isabella. You, Gabriella, and Leo deserve nothing but happiness, and I'll always be here to help you. Please be safe, and don't accept anything that's not all-consuming and encompassing."

"Thank you."

"Swear it."

"I iurare."

"Good." Retaking his straight stance, he smiles. "By blood and pact."

"We are one." *I'll do everything in my power to protect you all.*

I LEFT MY HORSE AND AUGUSTO AT THE HOME WE OWN CLOSE TO THE werewolf kingdom after a quick bath. My instructions are simple: if I'm not back within twenty-four hours, head back home and prepare for our return. Leo's also going to need him. No one will protect him better, especially with how uncertain I feel toward Uncle Roberto.

He loves us, but his past deeds have left a sour taste in my mouth.

His beliefs will clash with our future.

Two choices, and one will lead to bloodshed and heartbreak.

Besides, our parents still need to be laid to rest, and all their children will be present.

Coming to a stop by the large sequoia from our dream, I place my hand where gouges should be. Where his need for me drove him to embed those black-tipped claws deep into the wood before gripping my thigh and hoisting it over his hip.

The memory pulls a shiver from me. Deep and carnal, the need for him blooms and I take a moment to collect my breaths. The place looks different in the late evening sky, the trees almost swaying for me to a rhythm only they hear.

Welcoming. Home.

Beyond the large cluster of trees is another bush and then the lake. I can hear the water falling from the small cascade near the opposite end. Nothing large, but serenely pretty and soothing with its slow rolling waves and the flora that surrounds it.

A mini oasis.

Stepping through, I remove my sandals and carefully sit on the shore, mindful not to dirty the all-white dress I'd worn for Xadiel. And fuck, it feels so good after my long travels. The water is warm even though the temperature is a smidge cooler today. At least, cooler than it is back on Italian soil.

Wiggling my toes, I close my eyes and wait.

Yet behind my lids, I replay the vision from a few hours ago. The second I stepped foot onto the port.

A tall wolf in a sandy blond color steps out from the bushes to my right. He's strong, this one, with an aura that commands respect, but he is no alpha. Not a leader of another pack, and I immediately recognize him for what he is.

Family. A part of me.

So does the animal.

Head tilting down, he appraises me through pure-black orbs before lowering himself to the ground, belly and muzzle. This is a sign of respect. His thoughts are also open to me, and I find no malice within.

Instead, there's a connection formed. Innocent and honest.

Luna. Our queen.

The rustling of foliage greets my ears, and my eyes snap open. Waiting.

Not that I'm made to wait long. Just like in the vision, he comes through and his stern expression changes the moment our stares align. No malicious intent, but more of a realization. As if he doubted, but now understands—accepts me.

No question or hesitation.

Our connection snaps into place, strong and unyielding, but not in a romantic way. No. This tether he can't see is one I recognize;

brotherly, it's a few shades darker than the azure of Leo's and just as formidable.

They say lunas are motherly and defensive over the members of their pack.

I believe it now. Feel it.

Suddenly the cracking of bones fills the silence, and out of respect I turn my face. I'm not sure if he's mated or not, but I am even if mine doesn't want me. Even if I know the time will come and truths will be revealed.

"Luna?" a deep male voice says. I face him again, and now he's clothed in a pair of trousers and thin undershirt. He's also kneeling before me. Not too close, but just enough that I get a hint of his lemongrass scent. "Are you okay?"

"I am...?" I trail off, needing his name.

"My apologies...?" He does the same, waiting for me to start the introductions while holding a hand out toward me, and I take it, letting him tug me up. I'm on my bare feet before my next blink and wincing when a small pebble embeds itself in my left sole. He notices this, and before I can reach down, he's grabbing my belongings and handing them over.

I shake my head in amusement, taking them. "Isabella. Please call me Isabella, *not* Luna."

"Of course, I *will*, Luna Isabella." A snort escapes me and the man laughs.

"Clever and stubborn?"

"Guilty." But then the amusement vanishes, and I'm left with a man who's unhappy with the reason he's here. "Isabella, I'm sorry."

"For what?"

"I'm Gamma Cain of the Royal Evergreen Pack, and I'm here to—"

"Escort me." Not a question and he nods. "To Xadiel."

"Yes. Alpha wants to see you in his office."

11
ALPHA
XADIEL

There's a literal snap in me the second I enter my office.

I'm restless.

Pacing from one end to the other within minutes of Cain's message while Bartolo's beaten form lies unconscious in the next room. That confrontation will have to wait a little longer. The wolf's excitement can't be contained—his claws raking the inside of my skin, wanting to be let out—and a growl slips from my lips.

From angry to visceral hunger, the switch has been flipped and I need her here.

To see her again. Nothing else matters.

He remembers the hunt in my dream, and so do I.

How it felt to have her close and taste her lips.

Out, I say through the mind link, my tone rough. Near volatile. A warning to those close to my office or working inside the house; I want them all gone before she arrives.

Not because of what she is, but who.

That woman is mine, even if claiming her is an impossibility. Jealousy and possessiveness overtake my senses. I'm angry at Cain for being near Isabella—escorting her here—and his mate is the only reason I haven't shifted and challenged him for the right to walk beside her.

I hate it. I want her.

Can't control this need burning me from the inside, and it worries me. *How much is this reaction the animal?* Or am I weak? Controlled by lust and need and the sudden itch to bury my fangs in deep, tearing through muscle, so my mark can never be erased.

Not by me. Her. Or magic.

Footfalls exiting greet my ears a few seconds later, and I exhale once the last body leaves. My father isn't here or he'd have questions, but then again, he's never around anymore. Most of his days are now spent withering away in the library with old textbooks in a language I'm not versed in.

The strong and invincible man I grew up with is gone. A shell of himself.

Won't deny I miss our relationship, but we've handled Mum's death in different manners.

I want the heads of her killers. He wants to fade into the background until death arrives.

Both understand and hate it because right now duty and revenge take a back seat to a different kind of desire as a door near the back of the house opens. I pause, ears picking up their movements, one light and the other brusque, as they come closer.

Neither speaks, but the presence of one is strong, and it's mine.

Each steps has my chest rising and falling faster.

Then the scent of jasmine hits me like a battering ram and I stagger for a second, my cock giving a hard jerk behind the teeth of my zipper. I'm throbbing; a bead of pre-come beads at the tip, and I feel it slide slowly down the thick shaft a second before there's a knock.

Cain's not with her, and I'm thankful for that.

Where he went, I have no idea nor do I care because a second later, I'm pulling her inside. Isabella gasps at the sudden movement, stumbling a bit, but then her back is against the door and our eyes meet. Immediately, I'm lost to the mate pull. Overwhelmed by her and the way she takes me in.

Our bond is strong. More than I ever imagined.

She sees the beast inside me rise, his onyx eyes mixing with my gold, and the scent of her arousal causes a deep rumble to build inside my bare chest. The proof of how I affect her is pure pleasure to me. Like an aphrodisiac.

I want to hear her. To taste it.

Isabella is beauty personified with flaming red hair, baby blue eyes, and the sweetest lips I've ever seen. They're cherry red and plump, parted as she takes in a deep breath and then shivers. In a subtle way, my mate is scenting me and it's the sexiest thing.

How she moves closer, rubbing herself against me with small gyrations or the way her hands pet my chest. Stroking absentmindedly, her fingers dig in deep while her every exhale caresses my skin.

Then there's her body in that dress. *Motherfuck.*

White and sensual, the tight bodice molds to her perky tits and flat stomach while a lattice up the front exposes just enough to tempt a bloody priest before two high splits, one at each hip, gives me access to her supple thighs.

Her legs are perfection.

Her soft skin is incomplete without my spend marking her flesh.

My eyes devour every sinful inch, and the limited time on the lake—that dream—didn't do her justice.

"Fuck, Little Moon. What you do to me," I groan, towering over her, and it's something I'm finding myself enjoying. How tiny she is compared to my seven-foot frame. How she cranes her neck back to meet my heated stare, azure eyes that are full of so much want—longing. They're sparkling with desire, and I can't help but wrap an arm around her waist, lifting Isabella high enough for her to feel my cock against her mound.

Nose to nose. Mouths hovering.

Yet it's when she feels me there, hard and throbbing, that a tiny mewl leaves her. The sound is low, almost kittenish, and it's one I'll never forget. It's also the way her delicate features tighten just a smidge, as if the pleasure is too much, but then it smooths and her lips lightly touch mine.

"Xadiel." One word. That's all it takes.

My name from her lips is a decadent prayer, and I submit to her desires. My mouth slants over hers while my hands explore from her knee to hip, my touch light while memorizing the softness of her skin. The openings on each side give me access to all of her, exposed and at my mercy, and I don't hesitate to wrap her legs around my waist.

They squeeze me. Tremble.

Her wetness coats the front of my trousers and my nostrils flare, grip tightening on the bare skin of her upper right thigh. My other hand traverses higher, over her ribs to the underside of her tit, teasing the fabric-covered skin with two claws. I didn't realize they'd come out but enjoy how she reacts...

Goose bumps. Eyes closing. Chest arching and begging for attention.

"Say my name again, Isabella. I need to hear it," I groan into her mouth before sliding my tongue over hers, flicking and sucking the same way I'll devour her pussy. How I treat the beaded tip of her nipple, tapping the left one to the rhythm of her breathing. Each flick pulls little moans from her, the sound so beautiful. "Say it."

"Xadiel, I need—" she says but then stops, whimpering as the hand on her leg traces a little higher, pausing close enough to her pussy that if I extend my pinky, I'd touch her clit. And I do. Slowly, I trace the bundle lightly, featherlight and careful not to cut her, but the thought isn't an unpleasant one.

There's no doubt in my mind Isabella's blood would be sweet. Delicious.

Pulling my mouth from hers, I exhale roughly against her skin before dragging my short beard from her lips to her ear. "Do you want me to stop?"

"Gods, no. Need."

Low. Sultry. Wanton.

I want to hear her beg in that same naughty tone.

"Then tell me what you need, Isabella? Never hold back from me." Dragging two fingers through her slick folds, I part them before circling her tiny hole. It flexes, her core tightening in need, but I ignore the temptation. There's something I must do first. The animal and I thirst, and I nick the soft flesh next to her clit. Two small cuts, one on each side.

She winces but doesn't cry.

If anything, my female gets wetter.

Her juices coat my fingers, sliding down toward my palm, and the scent of her arousal is heady.

Makes me feel like I'm a god. I'm her world.

And that fills me with more pride than anything I've accomplished in my lifetime.

Not being a king. Not leading us through a war.

This moment cements what I was born to do.

"Xadiel, more." A choked gasp, her pelvis tilting in offering, those luscious thighs trembling on either side of my waist. There's something on one of them, a marking, but I'm too far gone to the pull—lust—to give it my full attention. *Later.* "I need more."

"So fucking beautiful, my female." The deep rumble reverberates through me to her, and Isabella's eyes roll back. She likes what I am. Wants the beast. "Will you behave while I get my fill of you?"

"Please."

"I like that word on your lips." Gripping the bare skin of her thighs, one in each hand now, I lift her high and smirk at the squeal she emits. She's tiny and light, so easily bendable, yet the moment I push the front of her dress up and expose her cunt, everything fades.

Her scent entraps me, and my wolf rises to the challenge.

Little moon is a hair's breadth from my lips. She's soaked and clenching with need; I take in her pink flesh and small entrance, almost feeling bad for her. Almost, but don't. If anything, I love it—knowing that when I knot her—she'll be unable to do anything but whine and shake in pleasure. That when I pull out, my mate will feel me for days after.

Isabella will be locked and full of my seed before the night is through.

The thought pulls a thundering groan from me, and she shivers, unaware of my plans for her.

I'm well above average; thick and long with an expandable sack at the base that will lock me deep inside her pussy. My spend will fill her to the brim, but my cock will hold it inside and make sure she's bred. That my pups will grow inside her.

Another mewl from Isabella and my nostrils flare.

I've never touched a woman before, but instinct is a marvelous thing.

One my wolf and I are in tune with, and that first slow lick is one I'll never forget. My female is soft and sweet, sugary with a delicate tang that comes from her blood. She's also untouched.

I will be her first. Her last.

The combination of these discoveries makes me ravenous, unable to take it slow, and I eat her like the animal I am while placing one of her legs over my shoulder.

My trousers tear at the seam with one savage tug.

I'm past rational. Past giving a fuck about propriety and palm my cock, stroking in time with each lick as my knot expands with the need to lock in deep. Fast, then slow and hard—adding pressure where she whimpers or cries out—thrusting into my tight fist while electricity shoots through my body wherever we touch.

Skin on skin, I revel in each pulse of our bond and the rightness that fills my chest.

Then, there's the purr that's only for her. Spurring Isabella to continue canting those hips as far as my hold allows and feed me the slickness mixed with her life's essence. The flat of my tongue collects each precious drop, but a few slip down and onto her arse.

That won't do.

Moreover, in that moment I almost understand vampires. The taste is an aphrodisiac—nirvana to me.

"What're you…oh *fuck*!" That moan is lovely. I need another.

Releasing my dick, I retake my grip on both legs, piercing the flesh with the blackened tip. She's pressed firmly against the door, thighs pinned and in the perfect split position. Isabella can't move, and I feast on both holes. From the rosebud of her arse to clit, I lave each with broad strokes of my tongue before pulling the trembling bundle between my lips.

My cock bobs with pleasure, and I feel the drops of pre-come slip from the slit. Her magic surrounds us and it feels like a caress, sweeping from my heavy balls to the underside and back again.

A torture I return with fervor.

I'm sucking and nipping, something my little moon likes, and the proof of it's on my tongue as another rush of wetness coats it. She's shaking, lips open yet no words come out but her eyes are bright and on mine. Never looking away. Letting me see all of her.

Isabella tries to gyrate then against my mouth but can't, and I can tell she likes it. The dominance. The noises her beasts make and how easily I control her pleasure.

It's all I want. To taste and give and gorge myself on the reward after.

"Give me what's mine, female." My fangs descend, the audible click causing her eyes to widen. For her chest to release a shuddering breath. "Come for me."

"Xadiel, I'm—"

"Going to listen to your mate like the good girl you are." Not a question, and she complies when I graze her clit with the tip of one fang. That's all it takes and she lets go so prettily, soaking my lips and chin, drowning me in that heavenly scent of jasmine and her sweet come.

My reaction is automatic. Near savage.

Before she realizes what's happening, her legs are dangling off the floor and the skirt of her dress is caught between us. My arm is curled around her waist—teeth are at her neck. The flesh there smells so good and I lick right over her pulse point, the vein throbbing against my tongue while my chest rises and falls fast.

Mark mate. Break her skin.

"You're mine, little female. I'll always treasure the innocence you saved for me." The words leave me on a gravelly tone a second before I bite down, breaking the skin, and that first taste of her blood, pure and decadent, brings everything into focus.

The jerk of my cock and the come shooting from the tip and onto the juncture between her thighs. I'd lost myself to the mate pull. Pinned and legs closed, I was thrusting between them while using her wetness as lubricant. Then, there's the sense of completion that boils through me, clashing with betrayal, and I rip my teeth from her neck, leaving behind cut flesh.

The imprint of my teeth is visible, yet somehow, I didn't penetrate deep enough.

"Xadiel?" Isabella asks, her voice shaky while reaching a hand out toward me as I step back, dropping my hold altogether. She stumbles a bit but doesn't fall. Instead, hurt settles across her features before she rights herself. There's also anger in her blue eyes, so much of it my chest aches, yet I ignore it.

"What did you do to me, *Witch*?" I sneer, spitting the last word with venom, angry with myself for losing focus and forgetting what she is. Who her mother is. "Answer me."

"Do what, *Wolf*?" Taking a step forward, she matches my stance.

Even her anger is attractive, and I hate her all the more for doing this to me. For being the gift, the moon goddess made mine. "You attacked me. You touched me."

The wolf whimpers in my head; he doesn't like seeing that she's upset. More so, with us.

Yet I don't stop. It's too much and my emotions become tumultuous—wrathful—as Mum's dead body flashes through my mind. How much pain this caused my family and kingdom. The threat Bartolo made not an hour ago.

"Whatever this was ends here." Fur sprouts across my limbs, the animal within fighting for control. *Stand down.* This bond will not control. We can't be. "I, Xadiel—"

"This was your third chance, Alpha King Evergreen. No more." Not Xadiel, but Alpha King, and the connotation to the title is acerbic. Hurt. Isabella's not looking at me; her shining eyes are trained somewhere over my shoulder. There's also no anger in her tone, but even if I want to respond, I don't. Can't. "Now I have a promise to fulfill."

I'm frozen as I watch her exit the room.

I'm unable to so much as say her name.

Yet one thing does break through, and it's my beta.

Alpha, Bartolo has escaped. We can't find him.

90

12
Isabella

A ferocious roar rocks the walls all around me as I search for a way out. I'm hurt and alone, and the physical manifestation of his true emotions burns me. The wound stings, and I feel the trickling of blood as he didn't seal it with his saliva—know it will heal without any signs of it ever being there.

My promise was not in vain.

And as much as it kills me to do so, I reject this bite. Him.

He bit me in the heat of the moment and not because of love—acceptance. What's more, a part of me knew this would happen, and yet I'd let my heart rule over common sense. Two paths, and one comes with tears; Xadiel doesn't want me—a truth I have to accept now.

Maybe this is my road to peace. To a life of solitude, yet freedom.

Rejections after being accepted by both parties, even while frowned upon by our kind, can be surpassed with time. There will always be a hole in my heart, a piece of my soul missing, but I will get past this.

I vow it.

"Luna Isabella," Cain says, appearing out of nowhere as I enter the kitchen. We came in this way earlier and he cuts me off a few feet from the door, blocking me as I try to walk around him. He's respectful not to touch me and the concern is real, almost enough to make me smile. I can't, though, not while my heart is shattered. "Are you okay?"

What did you do to me, Witch?

Whatever this was ends here.

"Yeah." Swallowing hard, I school my features. Bite the inside of my cheek to stop my lips from trembling. "It's getting late and I must get back."

"Back where?" he asks, but his eyes are on my neck. Then on my face. Back and forth, he shifts his attention while his features pinch tight. "You shouldn't leave like this."

"But I am."

"Please, Lu—" he starts, but my glare cuts him off. I don't want him to use the title; it's not mine. "I'm sorry, Isabella. I don't know what happened, but I ask that you don't leave like this. My wolf and I are worried. Traveling the woods at night is dangerous, more so past our borders."

"I'll have protection."

No elaboration needed, and he nods. They need to know I'm not alone. "Just one night."

There's a sudden glazed-over look in his stare before I can decline. Cain's looking at me but not here, and it dawns on me he's communicating with someone. His fangs drop the longer the exchange carries; I take in his defensive stance, lip curling over, and I take a step back.

Then another. And again.

The door is close enough now that I turn, but before I can touch the handle, a large body presses into me from behind. By the scent, I know it's Xadiel. Dominating and overwhelming, he encroaches on my space before flipping me around.

Cain is gone when I do. More than likely because of the man huffing before me, but I refuse to acknowledge.

"Look at me." A growl. Command.

"I suggest you move, Alpha King." I'm trying hard not to lash out. To control my abilities, and while I don't want to hurt him as he's pained me, my magic wants to protect. The powers gifted to me at birth are an entity on their own. They feed off my emotions, and right now they want to strike.

"No."

"It wasn't a request."

"Not until you tell me where he is."

"He who?"

"Lying to me will only make this worse." My lips part to respond, bitter curses on my tongue, but then I'm upside down and watching the door move further away. It takes a moment to understand Xadiel threw me over his shoulder, and even longer to realize we're heading up a set of stairs.

But then I'm fighting, kicking my legs and punching him—nails digging into his muscles where I find a tattoo. To be honest, I've been so distracted the last few times in his presence that I didn't pay attention to the markings, but now I am.

There's a crest on his back that takes up the whole expanse.

It's beautiful; a black wolf inside a shield with a crown atop its head, all in black and white. The animal is majestic, a replica of the one on my thigh, and I feel a deep connection to it. I'm unable to look away from him. The symbols on either side of him don't matter, and a second later I don't have the chance to decipher them anyway.

Now, we're face to face. Xadiel's bending a little at the waist to be on my level while his glare cuts through me like a lash from a spiked whip, and yet neither of us speaks. The silence stretches between us, and I'm more than uncomfortable; I want to run from my mate.

It's a need, a pulsing tick that grows louder and harsher the longer I take in his scent.

Don't leave, Isa. You need to be here.

A shift in the room makes me swallow hard for a different reason. Xadiel's talking to me, but I've gone mute because I heard her. That voice in my head isn't mine, and yet I feel it's familiar. Whoever the woman is, I can't deny her. I'm compelled not to, and it has nothing to do with magic or spells.

This is familial somehow.

"...you're staying here until I find him, Isabella."

"Okay."

I've surprised him, but that's the end of the conversation as a second later he steps into my space and tips my face up. His confusion is palpable. His desires are felt so deep within my marrow, yet I don't respond.

Not to the soft sweep of his knuckles across my cheek.

Not to the gentle press of his lips to my forehead.

Both actions mystify me; it throws him off too, as if done unconsciously, but then he smiles and my heart flutters. It's small yet genuine, but I don't return it. Can't.

"I'll be back, and we'll talk." His rough exhale sends shivers down my spine; the subtle taste of him in the air makes my mouth water. "This is unfair to us both. I know that, but wait for me here... that's all I ask."

"There's nothing to talk about."

"There is. A lot more than you think." With that, he leaves and the door closes softly behind him. A second later, the audible click of the lock engaging catches my attention and then the muted sound of him exchanging words with someone; I cross the room and turn the handle but nothing happens.

He locked me in.

I could leave. Gods, it'd be so easy to open a portal, yet I don't.

All because of that voice and message.

This goes past clearing my parents' names now. Something is toxic in this place.

I'VE BEEN LEFT TO MY OWN DEVICES FOR MORE THAN FORTY-EIGHT hours now. No food outside of a bowl with a few apples and grapes inside, plus the carafe of water beside it. They were on a table when I arrived, plenty of both, but they've dwindled quickly.

The room itself is nice: a large suite with a full bath that I've taken advantage of twice now. It's opulent with its rich green color and gold accents, and expensive fabrics hang from the window while a huge four-poster bed takes up the center.

But it's not his room. Of that, I'm sure.

This one has a feminine touch that's soothing, and I like it. Gives me a small sense of comfort through turbulent moments.

I want to leave and never look back. I want to fix whatever is breaking him.

There's also the fact that his scent is everywhere—embedded so deep within the walls.

So rich. So thick.

Almost as if he's nearby. Taunting me. Messing with my head. It's been like this since he locked me in here, and exhaustion is beginning to settle heavily. I'm cozy and warm for now, two defectors in my current yawning escapade and yo-yoing thoughts.

"I need a nap." My voice echoes throughout the room, losing its volume until disappearing into the quiet. "I'll decide what to do after."

ELENA M. REYES

Something is wrong in this place.

On these lands.

And now that I've been out of the mental fog Xadiel creates with his touch, I sense the sharper strands of deceit and dark magic. Just like when we rescued Meera, there's an enchantment to keep others out, but something calls me closer.

Fingering the hem of the dress I'm wearing, one I found inside a large wardrobe—a little small and tight, especially in the bust—I tuck my knees to my chest and close my eyes. I'm torn, finding myself emotionally drained the longer I'm here, but what choice do I have?

What if I'm here to save an innocent?

I can't walk away knowing someone is hurting. It goes against my beliefs and who I am.

Another yawn escapes, and I give myself a nod. I'll figure it out. All I need is some sleep.

I'M TORN FROM MY SLEEP BY AGGRESSIVE HANDS, A SCRAP OF FABRIC over my eyes. The scents are strong and wrong, dirty and make want to gag, but I stay calm. Don't make a sound, like my parents taught me.

It's easier to disarm the enemy when they don't know what you're thinking. Emotionally you can give away a lot.

They rip me from the bed, forcing me to my feet while placing heavy metal rings around my wrists that do nothing to me. I'm allowing this to happen. Each one locks into place with a loud, audible click, the sharp edges digging in and breaking the skin before I'm forced to walk. Each step stings. Their touch on my arms makes my stomach cramp.

No one speaks, though. That's fine.

Their breathing is heavy, yet controlled.

There's one presence, though, that is stronger in the group. A

96

leader, but he keeps his distance and watches, yet his aura is tinged with malicious intent. Darkness and envy. *Magic.*

I want to question him. Demand answers, but then we're descending the stairs, and growls pick up in volume. Multiple wolves, and they're angry—loud and close. Volatile, and warning me with the sound that they want my blood.

That I'm the enemy on their land.

We don't stop until we exit a door and walk out into the early morning air. A man on either side of me, hands gripping my upper arms tightly, and two in the front and back. I'm counting the different set of steps.

The breathing patterns. The individual scents.

I might be complacent now, but I'm not weak. Can defend myself and torture, too, if needed.

Besides that, there's the hint of light coming from the bottom edge of the fabric covering my eyes, just enough that I make out the forest floor and what looks like a cabin up ahead. At least, that's what I think it is after walking for a while. The structure is older, a little unkempt, and far enough from the royal manor to be undetected.

Why didn't I see this coming?

No warning. No vision. My mind is blurry today.

Inhaling deep, I calm myself and don't react. They can't stop my magic, my wrath, but keeping a level head will help them more than me.

Taking a life is Gabriella's forte, but she's taught me enough to disable if needed.

Plenty can happen in a few seconds.

The door opens, and a pair of high-heeled feet come into partial view. And still, no one talks, but I sense jerky hand movements before I'm ushered in and straight into another room. Darker. Colder.

These floors carry the weight of pain and blood. The structure weeps for the lives lost.

Someone snaps their fingers, and the shackles on my wrists are attached to a chain on the wall, my feet too. Heavy, the metal clangs before all males exit and two people remain.

"Good morning, Witch," the female voice says, her hand gripping my face a second before the blindfold comes off. Dim lighting bathes us and my eyes haven't adjusted yet, but it's easy to pick up the familial resemblance between her and Xadiel. She's not his mom, but a close relative and carries a smidge of mint in her scent. "Are you comfortable?"

"Who are you?" My voice is a little wobbly, but I clear it. "Why am I here?"

"My apologies." Her laughter grates on my skin. It's high pitched and fake. "I'm Theresa Evergreen, and this is the royal beta, Timoth."

"No last name?" Pinging my attention between the two, I keep track of their movements. She's dressed in a beautiful, floor-length black dress with delicate beading at the sweetheart neckline. He, on the other hand, is wearing a uniform that's almost military-like.

And both carry the stench of deceit along with something *else*.

What it is sits on the tip of my tongue; I recognize it but words fail me. Just like that film-like cover obscuring my gift of sight at the moment, it won't stay that way for long. I'll work through it.

However, I recognize it as ancient. Powerful.

"That's not important, Isabella Moore." Theresa's hand slips from my face, her nails leaving behind a few light scratches that will heal quickly. Most of the marks Xadiel left on me are already gone; all but the bite on my neck. That one hurts; I feel the heat coming off it.

"So you do know who I am."

"I do." Her tone is condescending as is her smirk, and both hide her disdain for the mark. How her eyes keep coming back to the red-tinged indent of his teeth on my neck. "But that's not what's important right now."

"You're right, love." Beta Timoth steps up beside her, wrapping an arm around her waist. The act pulls a giggle from the woman, who looks about fifty but could be centuries old for all I know. There's knowledge and pride in her eyes, but more predominant is the greed. "Nothing matters but the end game."

"You're not mates."

"How astute of you." Timoth looks at her as a coveted possession, and not the attractive kind. Like a stepping stone, and she's no better. "But you'll learn soon enough, little girl, that mates are worthless in the grand scheme of things. They get in the way and unfortunately, must be removed and replaced…just like you'll be."

"I'm not afraid of you."

"You should be," they answer in unison, but it's Theresa I'm focused on. Her parting words before exiting and locking the door behind them, stabs me in the chest.

Loyalty is a fickle thing, young child. My nephew will teach you that lesson—he'll be the cause of your tears and death.

13
Isabella

"You're on serving duty, *Witch*. Alpha's order." The man who introduced himself as the beta yesterday sneers, pushing me through an entryway and into a vast room filled with wolves. He'd collected me not long ago, almost caught me mid-dream walk—and dragged me through the forest and back to the estate with malicious intent clear in his eyes. Furthermore, I don't know if these people are part of the royal pack or not, but each member sitting and celebrating looks at me with disgust. So much hatred. "Get to work."

"No." The word is spit out with venom, yet the man is unaffected. Instead, he throws his head back and laughs while I glance around the room. It's large, easily the size of a ballroom with large tables throughout and chandeliers above each one. From one end to the other, the left side has windows that overlook the forest while the heavy, white linen drapes are open and tied to the side with an intricate woven rope the color of gold.

A crest sits at the center of each fabric panel; a black wolf inside a green shield with a crown atop its head, just like the one on Xadiel's back. This time, though, I make out the rest. On the left, there's the symbol of the sun and on the right, a moon with the Evergreen name stitched beneath each emblem.

The same one is found behind the raised dais where the royal table remains near empty, except for his aunt in all her overdone glory with a haughty look on her face. Triumphant. Cockier than our first encounter.

I've been in Theresa's presence twice now, spoken once, and I don't like her. Her spirit is dark; jealousy and gluttony exude from her while everyone remains aloof to it. I know it's because of my powers that I see and they don't, but the ugliness isn't hidden. More like no one pays attention because it doesn't affect them *yet*.

But it will. It always does with people like her.

Just like the longer I'm on these lands, my eyesight clears and what's been hidden rises from the murky waters. What controls the narrative is old, but not Wiccan. I know that now as I pick up the sharpness of a fae's enchantment—the sorcery is meant to create havoc, and it's done just that.

Theresa and Timoth are being led by it, but not against their will. This is deliberate.

What did King Larue offer them? Yet another thought is more daunting; he knows who my mate is. All of this was done to separate us.

Refocusing my attention on Theresa, I take in her appearance. She's in the finest silk dress the color scarlet red, not a hair out of place. There's jewelry on her neck, wrists, and ears as she smiles and waves at those in attendance. So many clamoring for her good favor.

You'd think this was a grand ball and not a simple dinner. Then again, I see many she-wolves in attendance dressed up with their partners in suits with ties that match their date's apparel. Xadiel's aunt still outshines them all, though. She wants the attention, yet not the kind I'll provide before leaving this place.

I will never beg a man. Not even my mate.

Will never allow myself to be treated as I have been ever again.

And had I not known better, I'd say she was the queen and not the aunt who's more than friendly with the beta. Their match is one of convenience and power status, not an ounce of love. Their auras don't linger or meld with one another. No complement.

My family never dressed like this to host coven dinners or meetings with sector leaders. We wanted our guests to feel comfortable and at peace while on our lands; Wiccan traditions are about connection and love, not opulence or false appearances.

He will be the cause of your tears and death.

"What did you say, bitch?" Timoth's hand strikes out and I step back on reflex, yet the shackles around my ankles impede me from creating enough space. He knows this and the gleam in his eyes confirms it, yet I don't back down.

Instead, I stare at him and wait for the strike that never comes, though.

Not so much as a graze to the cheek because I'm tugged aside while another werewolf steps forward in a challenging manor. "Touch my luna and die, Timoth," the males voice booms, the power behind his vow shocking those inside the royal dining hall.

Where did he come from?

The guests pause mid drink or bite, cutlery clanging against expensive china while the man who first stopped me while walking through their land grabs a hold of the beta's arm. One yank, and they're nose to nose, the younger of the two growling aggressively while taking a protective stance in front of me.

"Stand down, Gamma Cain. Know your place—"

"I'm not the one who's forgotten his bloody role in this pack, *Beta*," Cain snarls lowly, Timoth's title dripping with disdain. *Or maybe the feeling itself is for the man?* The two don't seem to like each other; it's clear as day in their eyes. Their body language. "She's untouchable by law, and I will not stand here and have you or anyone harm her."

"Gamma Cain," Theresa calls out, rushing over, the train of her red dress dragging across the rich wood flooring of the room. Gods, the wavelength of her true emotions hit me again, and my legs shake. It beats against my stability in this weakened state, but I stand strong. "What seems to be the problem here? Are you defying an order from your alpha and king?"

"Yes." No hesitation while those around us bare their teeth at that, snap them in our direction. All, except a tall woman who takes her place beside him. Their fingers intertwine and each gives a squeeze while their bond fills my chest with the first pleasant feeling since I walked out of Xadiel's office: true mates. "My vow is to the Alpha King and his *mate*, our Luna. Not one or the other."

"That's a treasonous stance you've taken, Gamma." Her cold eyes shift toward a set of guards coming closer. Not sure if they're here to stop the fight or grab Cain, but I breathe in deep and begin centering myself. I forget about the shackles and the soreness in my limbs—ready to protect us—but the near suffocating throb of a vision hits me at the most inopportune moment.

No matter how much I fight it, the scene before me flickers and a hidden room appears with a woman attached to a wall just like I'd been. She's older and unkempt, the frailty of her body causing my chest to constrict because her health is declining and fast.

Then, there are her eyes.

So much like those of the man who's broken my heart, and what's more shocking is how they're staring back at me. They're warm with hope and a near suffocating sadness; I swallow hard.

"Help me, sweet girl. Only you can find me."

She's the voice I heard a few days ago. Who told me not to leave.

However, I'm yanked from the vision by the sudden slam of the large, ornate doors. The wooden frame cracks upon the harsh impact, and a painting falls to the ground. Power radiates throughout the room, nearly crushing in its force, and every shifter bares its neck to the huge black wolf who's currently staring at me.

I don't bow, though.

Not for him. Not for anyone.

His chest rumbles and his eyes turn molten, the bright gold swirling with black as both man and beast take a step closer. Then another. Xadiel towers over every man in this room, his size so imposing that those who'd been serving drinks scurry out with their heads bowed so low they almost kneel.

Not that he pays them any mind. No. His heated stare is on me and my appearance, lips curling over his teeth while saliva drips from those large fangs. Teeth that have blood on them.

From head to toe, I'm taken in and King Xadiel isn't happy at the sight of my dirty white dress and the heavy metal around my wrists and ankles.

Displeasure. Anger. Yet the strongest emotion is possession.

It's lustful and fills the room as another snarl rips through his chest, causing many to whimper. They take a stand and step back, many now resting against walls and out of the way, expecting my bloodshed to paint the floors.

How wrong they are.

His ire isn't directed at me.

Yet I don't take my eyes off him in distrust. Not that I could if I wanted to.

The mate bond, while not fully established, is damming me.

The bite on my neck throbs once again, harsher this time, and I'm unable to control the way I react to his scent, woodsy with a hint of mint. Or the way his strength makes my thighs clench in need.

Being this close to him is a punishment. More so than being tossed inside that dirty room.

"Nephew, let us handle her. Don't dirty your—"

"Silence." Garbled and deadly, the single word leaves the muzzle of his wolf, and the stunned expressions around us cause me to take a step back. So does Gamma Cain and his wife, placing themselves now between me and their alpha as my mate is the biggest threat to my life. Not that it stops the animal who slowly begins to shift; bones snap and realign while the soft, thick fur becomes tanned, bare skin. His snout is the last to change, his sharp jaw and golden eyes forcing a gasp from my parted lips.

Why must he be so beautiful. A literal God walking among us.

Jealous energy fills me then, a consuming rage at the many eyes watching him, yet when I flick my stare around the grand room, I find something surprising. Females all around me close their eyes while their faces fully turn toward the floor. Even the men avoid our direction.

All except his family, the gamma, and a guard who rushes over with a pair of trousers in his shaky hands.

I hate the way him stepping into the bottoms and then tucking his thickness inside affects me. How the flaring of his nostrils and then low vibrations in his chest cause a rush of wetness to drip from my sex while at the same time soothing my emotions.

It's not fair.

I need to get out of here.

"Don't." For a second I think I've spoken out loud, but he's moved away from me while the gamma also snarls. I blink, and Xadiel's shaking form has Timoth by the neck, the second-in-command's toes barely skimming the ground while they're now nose to nose. "You have some explaining to do, Beta. What the bloody fuck is going on here?"

14

ALPHA
XADIEL

L eaving her locked in feels wrong.

Everything has felt that way since she walked out of my office, the finality in her vow striking a chord deep at the core of who I am. What I am.

Shifters believe in the moon goddess and trust her implicitly. She does not make mistakes; each soul mate is brought together to fortify and help you grow. To bring you joy, love, and humility where needed. Yet I've cursed her decision when it comes to my witch— tried to break us.

I've hurt her. Almost severed our bonds with a verbal rejection that would've devastated my wolf and her essence.

I'm an arsehole.

The truth in that stings, but I grit my teeth and continue down the set of stairs that lead to my private quarters. I ignore the curious looks, the flaring of nostrils as they pick up her lovely scent, and it takes everything in me not to snap at them.

An angry bark builds, a possessive wolf's caution, but I shake my head.

It's not their fault.

I've made mistakes and plan to rectify them. Get the answers to end all my doubts.

My elite guardsmen meet me in the foyer, waiting as I walk past them and head straight for the forest. These ten will come with me tonight, hunting the warlock, although I have a feeling this will be a short outing.

He was bloody and broken, unable to hold his own weight when I left him. There's no way he's gotten far…

Unless Bartolo had help.

Possibly more than one person, and Isabella wasn't one of them. That was clear when I mentioned his name and a baffled expression was her response.

At first, I'd blamed her. Can't deny it. It made sense at the time to put this on my inability to think past my need and her softness—taste —but then I looked into her eyes. His name meant nothing to her.

No twitch. No blink. Not a bloody sign of awareness.

All I saw was the hurt and the finality to forget me. To rip me from her very essence.

It's something I hate. Abhor the wrongness that lingers in the air between us.

"Shift and spread out. I want him found and back in the cells tonight."

"Yes, Alpha King."

My beast bursts forth mid-sprint, snarling into the early night sky while the pounding of paws disperses in different directions. Their minds are all connected to mine, their wolves hungry for the chase.

Slightly behind me and to the left, Cain's sandy blond wolf appears. His head dips in acknowledgement, and then he follows my lead.

He knows how I am.

Wolves are pack animals: live, run, and eat as a family. We need the closeness. Thrive in a cohesive unit.

And I enjoy it, too, except for when I hunt.

We do not share. We do not accept anyone so much as breathing in our prey's direction.

However, I make an exception this time.

The faster he's caught, the faster I get back to Isabella. Faster the inevitable confrontation can be put to rest for our good or destruction.

My steps thunder in the silence, the forest animals scurrying away while my nostrils expand: I'm trying to find a thread of his decaying scent, but there's nothing. As if the cloying essence never existed, but I stay on track.

"What do you mean he's gone, Timoth," I hiss from between clenched teeth, my muscles flexing as I fight to control a shift. The wolf wants the reins; he feels his female is in danger.

I have my doubts, though. She arrives, and now he's gone.

Once again, he thrashes against my hold, forcing my fangs to drop and muscles to expand—the thick black pelt of my animal growing throughout.

"Answer me."

"I'm sorry, Alpha. I found the room empty—"

"And what were you *doing here?"* No one knew he was here, much less had a reason to be inside the manor. My instructions were clear: every bloody person out.

I want no one near her. To hear her scream for me.

"I'd finished my run and after leaving instructions with the patrol leader, I came to talk with you. But the noises coming from—"

"Are none of your business."

"Of course, Alpha." Timoth's eyes pinch a little at the corner right before he rubs the back of his neck. *Out of annoyance or embarrassment, it makes no difference to me, but he's smart enough not to challenge me. I'd rip his head clean off if he did.* *"I'm not asking about your personal affairs."*

"Carry on."

"I'd turned to leave, but a glint caught my eyes. The door was wide open and this was on the floor. No sign of forced entry or his exit." Opening his palm, he shows me a small empty pouch and a golden dagger. The latter still has Bartolo's near-black blood on it. *"It's almost as if he vanished into thin air."*

"How do you know it's his?"

"The old scent of cloves clings strongly to it. Can't you sense it?"

Thin air. Untraceable.

But for some reason I can't explain, I sense what others don't. His imminent death—see the tendrils of his power as he uses it—but no other wolf can. And more and more I'm certain this is because of her.

I'm feeding off Little Moon's gift. Her Wiccan heritage that I cursed so much right now is a blessing and I expand my chest on a deep breath, exhaling the tension from my muscles and giving in to my baser instincts.

No human emotion. Not using logic, but I let my wolf take the reins fully.

Bartolo's here, of that I'm fucking sure. *I will find him.*

For three hours I scour every inch of the forest, running from east to west while Cain takes north and south. We check in with others, not stopping once to rest, but it's as I double back to an area closer to the royal manor that a breeze sweeps past and my head snaps to the left.

Along with ruffling my fur, it brings with it a light putrid trace of that stench.

There are two places he could be in that direction, and one is isolated. An iron gate surrounds the large structure, and only my father and I have access to unlock it. Dark within and lit by the sun or moon, my mum's greenhouse would be the ideal place to hide with its unattended interior and endless weeds.

But it's a disrespect. One I'll take a lager pound of flesh for.

He's at mum's greenhouse.

Howls sound in the distance. They heard me, and I take off at breakneck speed. Cain follows a second later, doubling back my way while his voice relays tactics to the others through our link.

We're going to corral him.

Spread out and in a circle, we begin to close in once fifty feet away. Stealth is key, to keep quiet, and I shift slowly. It comes with pain, the control to recede and reform at this reduced pace as the body fights to speed up, but my limbs realign with soreness.

The claws at my feet revert, and the large paws become feet. Fur recedes just the same as my tan flesh appears before my muzzle becomes a sharp jaw.

They stay the same. Wolves emerge in varying shades of brown and grey with Cain's standing out in a color near identical to his human hair. Low, they keep their bodies closer to the ground while their ears twitch and nostrils flare.

Ten feet from the entrance, I grab a pair of trousers from a hidden opening within a tree. They're tighter and smaller than my normal tailored bottoms, so much so that I don't zip them. All that matters is I'm tucked inside when entering Mum's building.

Who knows how long ago Mum placed this pair here. Something I never questioned in the past, the little things she did, because that's the kind of woman she was. Loving. Always taking care of others, and my chest aches as a flash of her decapitated body appears in my mind.

That anger I've been trying to hold back rises. A red mist overtakes my senses.

Another few feet closer, and a heart picks up its beats inside. Panic.

He knows.

"Stay. No one steps a foot inside." One by one, they give me a nod while I head straight for the still-closed gate. The warded lock is intact, no trace of obstruction, and I grab the key from a chain around my neck that's long enough to fit my wolf and human form.

It creaks, the sound loud, and I sense him trying to use his magic. Yet it fails him.

He tries again, and frustration mounts. Each emotion is clear for me to see, like a living entity, and I walk inside without pause.

Bartolo's on the ground, dragging his body deeper into the large room with empty clay pots and endless planting beds on either side of him. The further he moves back, the less lighting, and I enjoy his scream of terror when a second later I have my hand around his neck, his feet dangling a few inches off the ground.

His swollen, bloodshot eyes are on mine. His torn hands pushing at me, but I only tighten my grip until his face becomes ashen and his already split lips, turns a light blue.

No words are exchanged. None needed.

I carry him out and past the fence without a single word. Not until there's enough space between us and the greenhouse.

But once there is, I bring my other hand up and slash across his chest with my black-tipped claws. From just below his shoulder to the opposite side, I leave deep gouges behind with a smile. At once, he cries out and tries to cover the wound with his mangled hands, body thrashing in pain, and I revel in the sound of his screams.

By the neck, I bring us nose to nose. "Look at me." When he does, I'm met with tears and desperation. He's not healing as other witches do, his accelerated abilities failing him and every wound I've inflicted is gaping or infected. "I want the truth, Warlock. No more games."

"Killing me won't bring her back to you."

"Bartolo, I'm only just beginning."

PRESENT...

I'M ANGRY.

Motherfucking burning from the inside at the sight of her in chains and filthy, as if dragged through dirt. Someone had the audacity to put their hands on her.

Touched what belongs to me.

Because she does. Our situation doesn't change that, and it's the one thing the wolf and I agree on.

After Bartolo escaped and I locked her inside the luna's suite, I left to do what was necessary. She was meant to be safe in there. The personal fitting and relaxation space fit for what my mate is: a queen.

No one knew she was there. Just like no one was told Bartolo's unconscious body lay a locked door from my office. He wasn't fit to run away, his wounds too deep, yet the warlock still managed to escape without detection.

And while I left Timoth in charge, gave him my trust, the beta took advantage. Right now, he's the cause and catalyst where everything starts and begins. Two and two don't equate to four in this scenario; his explanations don't make sense the more I turn them over in my head.

Yet it was Timoth who reported him gone.

He also removed Isabella from her chambers.

The latter is indisputable with the traces of his scent lingering on my floor. He had no business there; an adjoining room next to ours designed with the sole purpose of my mate's comfort.

"Alpha, let's talk. What's the problem?"

A sardonic laugh escapes me at his idiotic question. "Where do I begin." Immediately, my attention slips to Little Moon and an irate growl builds in my chest. The sound is loud, reverberating throughout the large banquet hall, and many whimper. Not her, though.

Isabella sees right through me while I catalogue every smudge of dirt and the injuries on her wrists and ankles. Both look sore; my female is hurt, and that's unacceptable.

The one thing I'll never allow is Isabella to be put in physical danger, much less by my people.

I've done more than enough if my assumptions are true.

Remove those fucking shackles. Be careful not to hurt her.

Cain nods and moves to pull a key from his pocket, one that only the three highest ranks have, but before he touches the metal, they fall to the ground. Both sets. Isabella makes it a point to those here that she's no one's prisoner and she let them subdue her.

Why, though?

Since the stolen moments inside my office, the doubts have grown more. Morphed and turned like an invisible force that, coupled by the anger in her eyes, then and now, gnaws at me. Feels like a thousand-pound weight inside my stomach.

Have I been wrong?

I take a step in Isabella's direction with Timoth still in my hold, my grip cutting of his air supply, and she stiffens, her displeasure tickling my nose. I stop immediately, biting back the uncontrollable need to bring her comfort—to say something. It's the wrong time and I know that, but her emotions are mine. Even without trying, fighting this bond, it's grown and overrides everything.

Her reaction pains my wolf while I'm beginning to question those around me.

The warlock has refused to answer my questions no matter how he's tortured, but I see the change in him at the mention of her name. Something about Isabella and her sister, the mere thought of them, causes a high level of distress.

My acknowledgement of our mate bond.

How I can sense his imminent death.

All of it terrifies him.

I need them both in the same room.

"Answer me this," I hiss through clenched teeth, digging my claws deeper into his neck. Blood spurts from the gouges, landing on my face, and my wolf rumbles in approval. Her scent is still on him. His disgusting paws touched her. "Who the fuck told you to step inside my private quarters? To go anywhere near what's mine?"

15
ALPHA
XADIEL

"**W**ho, my king? I've disrespected no she-wolf."

Not denying he's been on my floor. Tainted our space.

Jealousy is an unforgiving emotion, and right now, it dominates my rationale. Wolves are territorial. Possessive, especially with our mates.

"Isabella Moore." Bringing his face close to mine, I retract my claws while ripping a piece of his flesh and then tossing it aside like the rubbish it is. He, on the other hand, scrambles back after meeting the floor. Closer to my aunt. "You overstepped, Beta. Put your hands on my mate."

Gasps rise from the crowd at her full name. A few whisper at my declaration.

"Nephew, what's the meaning of this?" Mum's sister steps tentatively closer to me and with a hand held out. She attempts to touch my arm but doesn't at the last second when I snap my teeth in her direction. "Xadiel, what's going on? This isn't like you."

"Don't." Volatile emotions swim within my veins; I'm more than ire. I'm a fire that's been stoked for too long, and my failure is currently smacking me in the face. I'm starting to see my mistake, at least where Isabella is concerned.

"My king, please." It's a mixture of a startled noise and high pitch, the shock on Theresa's face pronounced, but nothing pisses me off more than her stance. Almost irreproachable. "This is your beta you've attacked. A member of our family you're mistreating for a *witch.*"

Fear. Animosity. Challenge.

All three found in that one word.

One would think it's because her mate was killed by one or by the decree of a Wiccan royal, but not me. Her time of mourning lasted days. That's it. Since then, her attention turned to filling the position her sister held within the werewolf community, and I let her because I had no mate.

Isabella is a threat to that, even if I'm not sure where we stand.

If she's innocent—if I've been lied to—I've done my female a great disservice.

"I'd watch myself there, Aunt Theresa." I level her with a glare. "This isn't the time to test my patience."

"Xadiel, how can you speak to me like this?" Again, she shifts as if to protect Timoth, putting herself slightly closer, and my nose twitches. I catch his scent mixed with hers. *That explains his recent behavior, but how did I miss this?* "Have you forgotten what her mother—"

116

"Enough." My voice booms, cutting off my aunt's response. "Bring him in."

The reactions are immediate as Bartolo's mangled body is dragged and dumped at my feet by Grady and his son. They helped with his capture, as did Cain, who'd come back earlier with my order to escort Isabella to the underground cells.

His report back changed everything. They had undermined their king.

Many in the grand hall click their teeth at the prisoner. A few males begin to shake, their wolves wanting to burst free and exact revenge for their fallen queen, but one growl from me settles them. Heads lower and necks exposed, they still glower at the beaten man.

"Why are you bringing him—"

"Why is there a member of the fae guard here?" Isabella asks, cutting off my aunt, and her words cause Bartolo to freeze. We've tortured him for days, cut and bled him for hours on end, yet at her voice, he trembles. "High ranking at that."

"Are you sure, Isabella?" Voice gruff, I say her name and take in the automatic reaction. Little Moon swallows hard, a shiver running down her spine, and I like it. The beast does too, nearly purring for her, but I bite the sound back. Stop myself from moving closer.

Not now. Not until the truth comes out, and if she's innocent, I'll beg on my knees.

She'll deserve more than that.

"I am." Rubbing her sore wrists, Isabella steps closer while sniffing the air. It's delicate and cute, the tiny twitch. "He's fae, all right, but not the most dangerous one here. The stench on him is of death and not strong enough to hold any kind of enchantment."

"We can't trust her. These people are murderers," Theresa interjects, trying once again to touch me, but I sidestep her. Cut her with a look, and her expression shows hurt but also nervousness. She wrings her hands, eyes shifting around the room while Timoth's picked himself up and placed himself behind her. "Don't let her blind you. She'd say anything to save herself."

Cain mind links me the moment the last word slips past Theresa's lips.

Something smells foul, and it isn't the prisoner.

I agree and nod. Little Moon's calm demeanor speaks volumes to me.

Take your place behind my aunt and Timoth. No one leaves this room until I get the truth.

Yes, my king.

"Nasty Wiccan...son of a bitch," Bartolo cries out, back arching off the ground and she's barely moved one hand. She's saying something in another language, Latin I think and almost too low to hear, but you'd think she'd branded him with a red-hot iron with how he twists himself from the pain.

He's sweating and groaning, that dark blood seeming different now. There's a tinge of blue to it, small, but on the edges of each drop. It too is dark, a near navy tone but visible under the right lighting. *What the fuck?*

"Who put you up to this? Answer me." The power in her voice is unmistakable. Royalty. Isabella's looking at him, and there's so much hate in those clear blue orbs, but the determination outweighs all other emotions. Lips moving, her tiny fist closes and the older man grows ashen. "Why did Larue send you here?"

"Stop," he grits out, his unhealed hands clutching at his wounded chest. "How is this possible?"

"My sister taught me a few things." For a second my mate stumbles, knees weakening, but she rights herself before I can reach out and help. "Now answer me. Why are you here?"

"I'll never betray my master."

"Then die protecting that worthless scum."

Another imposing figure enters the room then, his thundering footsteps making my mate stop. All heads turn, and I'm surprised to see my father standing a few feet from me. His hands are shaking, claws extended out, and his sight is set on my mate. Anger comes off him in waves, permeating the room, but Isabella stands tall and unmoving.

Once again, she does not bow. She does not flinch.

"What is the meaning of this, Xadiel?" A few steps closer, my father stops beside me but softens when he gets a better look at my mate. No hostility. If anything, there's affection. *Hope.* "Isa?"

"Yes."

"Sweetheart, what are you doing here?"

"Long time no see, Mr. Evergreen." Isabella's tone is gentler, but her body language is still defensive. Untrusting. "And to answer your question, I came here, but that turned sour rather quickly."

"How so, young one?" I watch him take her in, not in a lustful way but rather fatherly. Yet the moment he sees her wrist and then ankles, his anger rises and his head turns in my direction. "What did you do?"

"I didn't."

"He hasn't," we say in unison. At that, she blushes for some reason, and I can't deny the color is lovely. Her embarrassment is sweet. "This doesn't matter right now..." Isabella holds her hand up, waving off his concern "...you have more than one enemy in your midst."

"Who? What's going on here?"

"Better question is why do you two mourn a woman who's alive?" Little Moon's voice is strong and steady, almost daring anyone to contradict her. Her eyes shift between my father and me, ignoring the shocked gasps around us and the hostile step forward my aunt takes. "Do you not feel her? Does the bond not sing for you?"

"I do, and it does."

Those words break me apart and my chest caves at the thought that it's even a possibility.

The feelings coursing through me clash, thundering in my veins while the organ in my chest constricts. For twelve months I've lived with a sense of complete loss—failure—that's near crippling.

I'd failed Mum by not being there when she needed protecting.

I'd broken my mate if it's true.

And what's worse, words fail me now. All but three. "Please prove it."

"That's why I stayed, Xadiel." No bite or reproach. Just understanding. "I've seen it."

At once, the room grows quiet. No one moves an inch, but I feel their stares. Anxiousness morphs into fear and then anger on behalf of their current and prior king. But it's two heartbeats I focus on, how they grow rapid in pace, almost frantic, and my mate isn't one of them.

Aunt Theresa and my beta are worried, the stench of the near panic tickling my nose.

"What did you see, dear child?" Father's tone is low yet firm. He walks closer to Isabella, but she holds a hand up and shakes her head. "I'm not going to hurt you."

"I prefer it this way."

"Don't believe her, James. It's a trick!" Theresa's cry comes a second after Grady grabs her arm, stopping her from attacking Isabella while Cain subdues Timoth. The latter tries to fight back, throwing a blow that connects with the gamma's chin but leaves no damage. "Let me go! What the hell are you doing?"

However, a second later the sound of a closed fist meeting a solid chest quiets everyone. "I've never stopped feeling her in here, Isa. The connection is small, every day buried it grows weaker, but it never stopped beating."

"That's because she's not gone. Hidden, but not gone."

"I know."

"You believe me?"

"Without a doubt. Your mother didn't kill my wife, Isa, and I've spent the last twelve months trying to figure out who did or where she is."

Nothing he could've said could cut me deeper than this. His trust in her family when I've searched for them with the intent to kill, to display her parents' heads on a spike at the entrance of my kingdom, will forever haunt me.

Your mother didn't kill my wife.

It echoes in my head.

Torturous. Damning me. If he's right…

Jesus. If it's true and Leonora Moore is innocent—I might've lost my mate.

My wolf's been subdued, content to just be in her presence, but rises at the thought. The half shift happens in a blink. My father calls my name while others move back, and I growl in his direction. My beast thrashes against my skin for complete control; he wants to claim her now—finish what I started—but then he calms. My human skin retakes its place, and all traces of him disappear.

One simple touch.

Just a graze of her hand and immediately I'm nothing more than a docile pup. Little Moon stands beside me now with her fingers embedded into the thick fur of my right arm.

She's not running them back and forth or tugging, but the heat of her palm is enough. It's soothing. Calms both of us because his fears are mine, too.

His throat clearing pulls her attention away from me, and I hate it. Want it back on me, but then I find a knowing look on my father's face.

A plethora of emotions flicker through him. Understanding and disappointment being the most predominant, and I know it's because of the unhealed wound where I tore her flesh. It's red and raw, and my teeth click to fix it. To lave the skin and heal her, but the way she quickly moves away stops me.

"Sorry." Another blush, and I swallow hard. "Where were we?"

"Don't be. All will be okay, my child." Dad smiles at her, the gentlest I've seen him since before Mum's death. Almost wistful. "By pact and blood…"

Something about those four words shake her. Pulls a deep, shuddering breath from her tiny frame before she whispers, "We are one."

16
ALPHA XADIEL

That weight on her shoulders seems to evaporate the moment she finishes, yet her body sags a bit and she touches her forehead, as if checking for a fever. I react on instinct. My arm is around her waist before she can complain or dodge me, keeping her tight to my chest while she heaves in large breaths.

"Please." That's all she says, but the need is so profound. The heaviness of her exhaustion cloaks her calming jasmine scent, and I nod against her head. Right now, she needs me to be what I've failed to before.

To put her before my need for the truth.

She knows where Mum is.

"Do you want me to take you outside for some fresh air?"

"No." She nuzzles into my chest, breathing me in deep. Every inhale relaxes her a little more, the rigidness of her muscles coming undone. "Just give me a second."

"Take all the time you need." *Cain, I want everyone out. Send them home except for my family and Timoth. They don't leave your sight. Understood?* "Let's get you off your feet for a bit, Little Moon. I'm going to pick you up now."

Another rough exhale. "Okay."

Your father already started. We'll be waiting in the kitchen, but what about Bartolo?

Send him back to his cell and re-chain him.

Consider it done, Alpha.

My eyes shift around the room and indeed find it empty. The door I'd broken earlier in my rage is half-closed, propped against the other while the lights have been lowered to a pleasant dim.

Thank you, Cain.

On the opposite wall sits the royal dais and I pick her up bridal style, biting back a grin at the squeak she emits. How she digs her fingers into the muscles of my shoulders, almost afraid I'd drop her. It's adorable, as is the way she blooms pink when I sit us down with her in my lap.

Isabella tries to stand up, shift away, but her lack of strength at the moment is to my advantage...and concern. With her this close, I get a good look at her and notice the dark bags under her eyes, how her chest rises and falls with rapid breaths.

"What did they do to you?" The urge to place her in a bed while I tear Timoth and whoever helped him limb from limb is strong—near demonic. "Tell me, and I'll bring you their heads."

"Why would you do that for someone you hate? For someone you locked in a room, too?"

"I don't hate you, little witch." At that she bristles, pushing my hands away but they don't budge from around her waist. "Never have, although I've tried. Without lifting a finger, Isabella, you've tattooed yourself on my skin."

"Let. Go."

"No." A glass of water sits in front of my placement at the table and I reach over, grabbing it before bringing it to her mouth. Isabella shakes her head, stubbornly refusing my care, and my wolf whimpers. The sound leaves my mouth and her eyes snap to mine, lips parted. "It hurts him when you push us away. All he—*we* want is to care for you."

"*He's* not the problem, Alpha King. You chose, and I keep my promises."

"Please call me by my name. Never my title, not from you."

"I can't. This is how it must be." This time when I bring the drink to her lips, she parts them and allows me to serve her. Each sip is slow, careful not to spill while I tear my attention away. So much is going through my mind: confusion, but the biggest of all is regret.

"Please let me open your eyes."

She pulls back, licking the solitary drop of liquid on her bottom lip. "You remember."

"I do." Voice rough, I clear it, hoping it erases my jealousy over that tiny bit of water. "I remember everything, even if I don't understand how it happened. That dream felt too real to be anything but."

"Magic is a wondrous thing…" Isabella huffs, lips pursing before nodding to herself "…Alpha Xadiel. That trick has come in handy. Mom made sure we were always prepared for the worst."

"Worst how?" I ask, even if at the mention of her mum I release a short growl and my nails extend, tearing a small hole in her dirty white dress. "Sorry."

"It's okay." The smile on her face is sad, those blue orbs having lost their shine, and I don't stop her this time when she taps my hands. I release her and she stands immediately, taking enough steps to create distance between us. "All our lives, my sister and I have been desired by those wishing to obtain power. Fake bonds were claimed, threats made, and lastly, people I love taken from me. I know how to dream walk because if we were ever taken, that's how I'd get help."

"I'm sorry."

"Not important anymore, but this is." Taking in a deep breath, my mate places her hands palms up over the left end of the table and stares straight ahead. Her breathing is even and her lips move, but I can't make out what she's saying. Once, twice...five times she repeats the incantation before her eyes become glazed over, and I'm able to see her aura spread. It opens and the light extends, moving throughout the room before stopping.

Her blue eyes blink rapidly, shifting toward an empty wall while the cutlery near her moves. Subtle, until it's not and one falls. The sharp clink brings her out of whatever trance she's in, and this time when she looks at me, I find hope.

True open relief because she's innocent, while at the same time restless dread.

I see it. Feel it. Choke on it.

"You're the reason I see what's not there. Why I could tell Bartolo was sick—dying—and noticed the darkness within him." Not a question, but it's a curiosity I can't shake. Need to know.

He didn't heal; injuries old and new look infected and have some measure of necrosis.

"As my mate, you're able to pick up on things you were blind to before. That's my magic protecting you."

"How does it work? Why?"

"Doesn't matter now." I go to protest, but she shakes her head. "She's alive and we need to find her."

"Isabella, you're—" I'm stopped by a cutting look; she's oblivious to the blood on her nose. It's a small amount, a few drips, but then she grabs her head and it's not the first time. This is draining her, and I feel like a right arsehole for wanting to push and ask her where Mum is now and how we find her. Swallowing past my emotions, I push my chair back and stand, rushing to her side when she sways. "Please sit. Take a moment to gather your strength."

"Not needed." Twitching her nose, she huffs and grabs a linen napkin, bringing it to her face. She wipes it and then tips her head back, grimacing the entire time. I hate her distress. The sourness of her need to get away from me—my touch. "This happens when I'm exhausted. I'll be fine with some sleep later."

"Please, you need to—"

"Find your mom." Had anyone else cut me off, I'd have forced them into submission, yet with her, I find it amusing. My wolf does, too. He likes Little Moon's strength, admires her beauty, even if concern is the predominant emotion when it comes to her. We're pushing her too hard. "She's here, and there isn't much time before the damage is permanent. Call them back."

"Are you sure?" This is selfish. *I'm between a rock and a hard place.*

Save one or hurt the other. Choosing is near impossible.

"Yes." Conviction. Honesty. "And please hurry. She's been kept in chains long enough."

PACK MEMBERS CONGREGATE OUT ON THE FRONT LAWN. THEY'RE waiting and praying, on their knees while the voices of many call out to the moon goddess for a miracle. There's happiness and hope in the air, but with it comes the light tinge of shame—anger.

The lies and betrayal hurt. We will never be the same after this.

"Bring me blankets, water, and find the healer. Tell her what's going on, and close the door on your way out." Grady nods at my command and exits with another shifter, Elton, one of the older elite ten. They're in here now, too, surrounding my aunt and Timoth who share nervous glances. "Where is she?"

"I don't know what she's told you." Aunt Theresa swallows, dusting the front of her dress. "You know this pains me, Xadiel, but my sister is—"

"The truth."

"Why can't you see that the *witch* is lying to you?" There are tears in her eyes, but they don't fall. Her bottom lip trembles, too. "They want us fighting. This is how they defeat you."

Not us shifters. Just me.

Nothing from the ex-beta, though. He's gone mute and reeks of fear, shifting from foot to foot.

"Last chance, Theresa. Tell me."

She never gets a chance to answer because a few seconds later Isabella moves toward the way she eyed earlier. It's across from the dais, in perfect view from me, and everyone turns to watch her move. Her slim hand skims across the stone wall, touching all crevices, and the closer to the bottom left she gets, Timoth moves.

One foot at first and then another, backing away from Theresa.

Put him on his knees.

Osmund, another elite, lands a swift kick, and the crack of a knee shattering is loud in the room. His cry follows, the curse of a pathetic wolf that I ignore. As his king and alpha, it hurts me to see one of my kind hurt, but his treachery can't be forgiven or ever forgotten.

So I walk away and stop beside my mate.

She's breathing hard again; I see the tremble of her hand. Her body sways and lips move, fingers skimming over a particular area and then her head tilts to the side and she taps a piece of stone. Just one light hit and there's a hollow sound.

It's low and subtle, but my ears catch it. So do the others.

"Found it."

Everything goes quiet. No one so much as moves, but my aunt tries one last plea. "Xadiel, please stop this! It's a trap...that Wiccan whore put it there to end you all."

"Silence." My command thunders in the room and all bare their neck; I'm in her face before she has a chance to move with my hand around her neck. Shock flashes across her face, a scream caught in her throat, but I raise my other hand to her mouth and cover it. Bring us nose to nose. "One more word about my mate, and I'll snap your neck where you stand. I won't warn you again."

"Son," Dad calls out and when I turn my face, there's an open door where a solid wall stood. The opening isn't large, the landing even smaller, but my mate steps through without pause. My father follows, the stairs leading them Gods know where and I do the same, releasing Theresa before pushing her forward.

"No one in or out. Cain, come with me."

"Yes, Alpha King."

Cain quickly falls into step before I'm in the doorway, but the howl of relief changes that. We're flying down the narrow stairway, forcing Theresa down first and she yells the entire time. Begging. Pleading. I ignore it all until we reach the bottom and come face to face with a heartbreaking sight.

My mother, frail and bruised, is in chains attached to wooden beams. They're silver; the burns on her wrist are red and open with a severe infection. She's crying, hiccuping breaths of relief while my father rips the bonds off and catches her in his arms.

He's whispering to her. Crying. And through it all, my mate watches them with a wistful expression. Happy yet sad.

She will never forgive me.

"Sister, what have they done to you!" Theresa reacts as one would expect, but you can't fake the way my mum recoils or the hatred in her eyes. Eyes that shift around the room before finding mine, her hand extended out toward me. "Do you not recognize me?"

"Take another step and I'll kill you," my father growls, warning her. Cain yanks my aunt back by the arm and pins her against the wall.

Get her upstairs until we decide what to do.

On it. And Xadiel, this is a blessing from the Goddess.

"My pup," Mum whispers, and I close the link, her voice hoarse and lips chapped. It's the sweetest sound and I'm beside her in an instant, placing my forehead on her shoulder while being careful of her injuries. Dad releases another howl, low and happy this time, and I mimic the sound. As do Cain and the others upstairs, billowing their joyful sounds throughout the house and outside gardens.

You can feel the palpable relief. The utter peace this brings our kingdom.

"Thank you for not leaving, dear child. For hearing my pleas." In my moment of celebration, I'd forgotten my female is here. What she's done for us, but Mum cranes her neck back a bit to find her near the wall. "Did Leonora send you?"

Utter sadness comes from Isabella. It strikes me fast and hard. Her emotions settle in my chest, and my head snaps in her direction just in time to catch a few stray tears roll down her cheeks. The smile on her face cracks the longer our eyes meet, but then she looks away and addresses the question.

"No. Mom didn't send me."

"She let you come here by yourself? Without protection?" Mum tries to stand, nearly pushing Dad away in her haste, and I'm pinging back and forth between the two. Something about Little Moon's response distresses her, and I don't understand why. Not until I meet my father's sorrow-filled gaze.

The same one he wore the day he thought he'd lost his mate. Loss. Grief.

Goddess, no. Please, no.

"We can discuss my parents at another time, Mrs. Evergreen. Let's get you out of—"

"Tell me the truth, Isa," Mum insists, shakily walking closer to Isabella with the help of her mate, each step slow and careful. "Where's my good friend?"

That's why I never found them. They're gone.

"I'm sorry," Little Moon chokes out; the trembling from before returns and it's magnified. I try to touch my mate, to calm her, but she pushes my hand away through blurry eyes. My female's head shakes from side to side, gasping breaths catching in her chest, and she fully leans against the wall for support. Concern comes from my parents—we're watching her, but then her eyes roll back and I'm catching Isabella. Hear the words that rip me in two for a different reason while my mother releases a wail. "They're dead."

17
Isabella

The scent of cedar and mint surrounds me, lulling me into a peaceful state between slumber and awareness that I don't want to let go of. My bones hurt. Every part of my body is sore, and moving means this serenity will be gone.

I know where I am. Who sits beside me and whose bed this is.

Xadiel Evergreen surrounds me on a molecular level; he's a part of me, and I'd find him in a room full of a thousand people within seconds. How that happened, I have no idea, more so because our mating isn't complete. The bite mark on my neck is proof of that, although it hurts less today than the last time I was awake.

"What happened? How long was I out?" I ask, refusing to open my eyes. It's better this way. His handsome face is a weakness. My body craves his. I can't control this pull—how strong it is within this close proximity—but distance will lessen the spiteful need. *It has to.*

"You passed out two days ago due to exhaustion and I healed your neck. I couldn't let you suffer anymore." A large, warm hand pushes the strands of hair on my forehead back, lingering over my temple, then moving from one side to the other. Skimming low on my cheek. "Scared the hell out of me, Isabella."

The sincerity in his voice shakes me, but I focus on my breathing, keeping the shaky butterflies currently residing in my stomach from showing, from seeping into my tone at the knowledge he tended to the bite. "My apologies, Alpha King. That wasn't my intention."

"Don't." Both his hands cup my face now, his mouth so close to mine, his breath caressing my lips. "I know I deserve this. What I've put you through is something I'll never forgive myself for—I expect you to give me hell—but don't treat me like a stranger. Hit me, bite me, curse me…but do it while looking at me."

"I never meant to worry you." Unwillingly, my lids open and I meet his golden eyes with the beautiful, black swirl. His wolf is here. Present in the low purring I don't think he's aware of making. The low vibrations run through me, settling my rising nerves and the small shaking of my limbs. *His effect on me is unfair.*

"The fact you're apologizing…" he trails off for a second, pained expression marring his sharp features while he swallows hard "…I failed you, my mate."

"It's been a rough few weeks, and I neglected the warning signs. Give me a few minutes, and I'll be on my way."

"No." Loud, the growl reverberates throughout the room. The command is felt, but I'm not moved to submit like werewolves do. Perk of being his equal.

"What do you mean, no?"

"You're not leaving me, Isabella." I'm quick to push his hands away at that, scrambling to the edge of the bed but I never make it. Not with this beast of a man moving me to his liking and situating me in the middle of the mattress this time; his hulking form caging me. His nostrils flare and eyes turn darker than I've seen to date, while the arms on either side of my head keep most of his weight off me. Most, because the heat is still there as is the gentlest touch each time he exhales. "I'm man enough to admit I've made plenty of mistakes when it comes to you, Isabella, but this won't be one of them. It's selfish of me, I know that, but I can't let you go."

"Just a couple days ago you would have." Every word is drenched in bitterness. My truth. I'm angry at him, how exposed this makes me feel. Not once did he give me the benefit of the doubt—let me prove my family's innocence, and now it's supposed to be okay? "Finding your mother changes nothing, Xadiel. You should've trusted me."

"You're right," he says, voice gravelly, before lowering his face to lay a tiny kiss on the tip of my nose and each cheek. Xadiel is scenting me, and I hate to admit, I find it cute. How he nuzzles into me, mixing his cedar and mint essence with mine, making sure others who come near me can smell it. Him. At the crook of my neck, he inhales deep and a rumble of approval greets my ears. This is how we lie for a while, just being, but then he speaks again so low I almost miss it. "I sinned against you, my female, and I'll spend the rest of my life paying that penance. All I ask is that you do it by my side. That you allow me to make amends."

"I need to go," I blurt out instead, and at once heat flushes my skin. It's not what I want, but what must be done. I'm not trying to hurt him, rather allow us time to cool down and think. Our lives are forever intertwined and eternity is too long to be angry, but that doesn't negate he and the werewolves here owe me the time to recover. Moreover, putting my needs before their own is how they—he—starts doing that. "At least for a while."

"Why?"

"Because my mother and father were never laid to rest. Not as they deserve." *Goddess above.* The sheer guilt and hurt coming off him feels like a tsunami slammed into my ribcage. This isn't what I expected. Regret, yes, but to actually grieve them lessens a little of my rage. Not all, but I do wrap my arms around his neck and pull him down to me. The hug is just as much for him as it is for me, the comfort settling my fatigued soul. "My siblings and I are coming home to pay our respects, Xadiel," I whisper, and he nods. "Our traditions require this so the deceased can rest and become one with the earth again. We've been running and hiding for so long, unable to do so, but now it's time. Can you understand that?"

"How long?"

"I'm not sure."

Pulling back just enough to meet my eyes, he gives me a small, resolute smile. "Can I escort you?"

"No." Witches have been hunted by wolves because of the lies fed by the fae king. The last thing I want is to scare those living on our lands—the women who've been hurt and abused by the same people who killed my parents. "Now isn't the right time."

"Then so be it." That's it. No arguing. Instead, he removes my arms and then gathers himself at the corner of his bed while I watch, unsure of what just happened. One second, he's not letting me go, and the next, he's holding a hand out to help me off the large, four-poster bed. "Would you be willing to say goodbye to my mum? She's been asking about you."

"Of course."

"Then come. They're expecting us in the grand hall."

WE DIDN'T HEAD DOWN RIGHT AWAY AS XADIEL PREPARED A BATH for me first; the large claw-foot tub filled to the brim with warm water and expensive oils was heaven. A new bar of soap, a washcloth, and small cup of tea all sat atop the tray near the edge and right by the faucet. The piece was large enough to extend from side to side and made of wood, the craftsmanship exquisite, as was the rest of the large bathroom.

One would think it to be sterile, the all-while motif stark, but there's warmth in the simplicity. From the white stone flooring to the walls and even the filigree work near the large window at the center all made the room inviting. Soothing. *Home.*

Can't deny it. Lying to myself is an impossibility.

I knew what coming here meant and what was at stake—my heart—but came anyway because saving him from the path of destruction is worth it all. My life. My powers, if it came down to it.

Yet it still stings. Xadiel will always be my greatest joy or destruction.

That was thirty minutes ago, and now, I'm standing beside Xadiel in a lovely off-the-shoulder floor-length dress in a light mint color. The material is soft and a bit ruffled, elegant and simple, yet the split over the leg without my tattoo shows just enough to be sexy.

I like it. A lot. So does the man beside me who hasn't stopped starting at me from the corner of his eyes. Not since he knocked on the bedroom door, the same one I'd been given by Cain a few nights ago, while holding a single red rose.

His groan of approval turned hungry growl rather quickly. More so because I'd refused to let him scent me again.

"Going home is the right thing," I whisper under my breath, yet he hears and stiffens, but then it's too late as the ornate doors open and all eyes are on us. Every single pack member from that fiasco of a dinner is in attendance, and the hostile attitude is gone.

I'm met with submission. With bared necks.

One by one, the werewolves drop to their knees as Xadiel leads me toward another dais, this time with four chairs, and the two at the center are unoccupied. His parents are already there, watching us with matching grins and Goddess, what a difference a few days make.

His mother looks healthier. There's a touch of pink on her cheeks, and it's not makeup. Instead, the glow comes from the way her husband sends subtle winks in her direction. From seeing her only child walk in and hug her once we're close a few second later.

They exchange words, smiles, but then both look in my direction.

Without noticing, I'm shifting from foot to foot at the step leading up, the sandals on my feet making a short clicking sound. My nerves are getting the best of me, and I want to leave. I feel the pinprick of a thousand needles rise across my flesh.

It's too soon to be back here, and I rub my wrist while meeting her eyes. Not his. "I think it's best I take my leave now."

Whimpers come from the werewolves; their distress eats at me.

I know what it means, and I'm not ready.

"Leave?" His mother's brow furrows, shifting her gaze from me to Xadiel. "Where are you going, Isa? Who's accompanying her?"

"I'm needed at home."

"But I thought you're his—"

"There's something important she needs to take care of with her siblings, Mum. Isabella will be back." Her son's tone leaves no room for argument, and I'm thankful she lets it go. Even if it's to stand up, her equilibrium is still shaky and her husband and Xadiel rush to help her, both grumbling when she slaps their hands away. The act is simple, but to see two men chastised by the petite woman is hilarious.

A giggle slips from me, and it's as if I physically breathed air into the room. At once it lightens and the oppressive cloak lifts, giving me the much-needed relief. As Luna, by desire or default, I have no choice in the connection that appeared the second their alpha and I met.

Every grievance. Every moment of joy. The needs and fears; I experience it all, along with this overwhelming necessity to protect and nurture.

Just like I sense their hesitancy in how to approach me. The need to ask for a forgiveness that I'm not ready to give. *All of this is too soon.*

"My apologies, your highnesses. Please blame it on—"

"I'd give my very soul to hear that sound again." Stepping away from his mother, Xadiel walks the three steps to me and holds his hand out. For a few beats, we just stare at each other, get lost in the magnetic pull of his soul calling to mine, before I place mine in his much larger one. His skin on mine feels like heaven, the pinpricks from before becoming a low electrical current that flows from limb to limb, leaving behind a pleasant tickling sensation. "Thank you."

"For what?" I ask, taking the offered seat beside his. It's not lost on me that I'm facing the pack in the luna's seat, that this is a big moment for us, but right now the honest affection in his golden orbs holds me captive.

This was all I ever wanted. To have my mate look at me like I'm his.

No hate. No doubts.

So why can't I let it go?

"My King and Luna, the prisoners are here," Cain says then, and the spell is broken. I look toward the gamma's direction and find two people at his feet, still wearing the clothes from a few days ago.

They're angry and glaring at me; I'm not the only one who notices this. Cain's mate steps behind Theresa and yanks her hair, forcing her head to arch back at an uncomfortable angle. Timoth, on the other hand, is forehead to the ground with a boot on his skull, lip busted and staining the light flooring in here.

The room is grand and opulent. A large hall meant for balls and gatherings—decorated with grand chandeliers, expensive stone flooring, and the royal crest hanging between each stained-glass window —from one end to the other.

"Treason is a high charge for any monarch, but we wolves are more than that. Pack is family. Pack is sacred." Multiple fists meet chests, men and women showing solidarity to their king. "This betrayal goes past hurting a sister, your past queen, but it's against each and every one of you."

"Lies," Theresa hisses from between clenched teeth. "All I've done is care for this pack."

"To your own convenience." Xadiel gives a nod to Cain's wife, and the latter pops his aunt's shoulder out of socket. No hesitation or remorse, and I understand him. If given the chance, my siblings and I would do worse to those who killed our parents. "Deny it now. I dare you."

Before she can reply, five more bodies are brought in: the fae soldier and four werewolves, each bound by silver.

They're beaten and limping.

Their scents are also familiar, and it takes me a second to understand why.

"They're the ones who grabbed me and took me to a cabin in the woods." The words slip out before I can stop them, and my mate's resounding snarl makes the room shake. In a flash, he has two of them by the neck, their feet high off the ground, while the others cower. Whimper with their faces now touching the ground.

"Why?" he asks the wolves, both trembling in his hold. "Answer me!"

"They paid us heavily to remove anyone in their way," the middle-aged one says, sweating profusely. "Your aunt and the beta made a pact with some fae royal. That's all we know."

"Are you sure?"

"Yes, Alpha."

"May you never find rest at the moon goddess's feet." His claws emerge and embed through the necks, from one side to the other, and both go limp. With the other two, he slices a gash from stomach to collarbone and kicks them aside. They're not dead yet. Wolves heal at alarming rates, but the silver binding their hands will prevent it.

Instead, they'll bleed out. Slowly. Painfully.

Bartolo's looking at him with hope for an end, to be put out of his misery. I see his desire to end it all, sense it approaching, but as I look further, my vision becomes blurry. Interrupted by someone, and they're in this room.

The hold isn't strong enough to keep its grip; it wavers after a minute, and my head snaps toward a thin figure by the back wall.

She's pretty; a blonde dressed in a maid's uniform but she doesn't belong here.

How do they not sense her?

Our eyes meet, and I catch the resemblance between her and the fae captive. Possible daughter or granddaughter.

"You," I say, but it's interrupted by shouts of joy as Cain is named the new beta and a few second later, Xadiel kills Bartolo. His head rolls away from the body, spraying the ground and Theresa with his blood, before it stops beside her thigh.

But I'm more concerned by another scene.

The blonde woman taps her head and chest, mouthing the words *vita lapis* before releasing a small amount of black dust on the ground. For a small moment, I catch the glint of tears, the pain of mourning, but that's gone before she cloaks herself and disappears from the room.

18
ALPHA
XADIEL

I've been following her through the woods and past neutral lands for a while now. She wanted to leave immediately after Theresa and Timoth were sent to the perfect holding cell—and while I understood her reasoning—I wasn't going to let her go on her bloody own.

I'm an arsehole for my part in the mess our mating became, but I'll always protect what's mine. Because that's what she is.

Since the first day, I've never denied wanting her or the chaos Isabella creates within me.

Even at my angriest, I couldn't harm her. It's physically impossible to do so.

Isabella said her goodbyes to my parents with affection and a few shared tears, more so when they finally discussed the passing of her parents. Seeing my mother cry at not being strong enough to endure the journey cut deep, but Isabella's tears and understanding tore me in two. Beta Cain and his wife also received a warm hug, while everyone else watched them with longing—with the desire to earn her forgiveness for their part in harming her.

She's not angry, just indifferent at the moment, and I know it'll come to a head. Emotions kept bottled up will eventually implode, and I'll take the brunt of her ire and worse, disappointment, when that time comes.

Because there's more to being my queen than the fancy title. Like me, she'll feel responsible for many, but where I'm the brute strength in this equation, she's the stability and emotional support were- wolves need. Not because I'm doubting her ability to fight or defend —she's more than capable—but because at her core, Isabella is everything good. My balance and moral compass.

I saw that when she pushed herself to the breaking point to save my mum. How she worries about her family and fought to clear her parents' names, no matter what she faced.

That kind of love is unselfish and pure.

I see that now. Her.

The goddess doesn't make mistakes.

A truth I'm being smacked with, and I repent for ever doubting her.

My mate is perfection. My other half.

Now to make her see I'm right for her.

Because the alternative is unfathomable.

A twig breaks beneath my paw and I worry for a moment she heard, but Little Moon continues walking through the forest without worry or fear. Doesn't so much as look behind her every so often, but I do catch the furrow of her brow.

Then again, I saw her make Bartolo a right bitch with the shift of her palm and a few words. How she handled him was sexy, her power and conviction more than admirable.

But I'm here now to lighten her worry. Ease her mind and be the pillar I should've been from the start.

It's hard, but I manage to bite back a growl when she bumps into a low-hanging branch a few minutes later, the ends scratching her arm. And for the tenth time tonight, I'm tempted to carry her on my back through this thick and dense area.

Where she's going? I have no idea, but we're not that far past the lake. Through a thick cluster of trees and open land with tall grass, her bare feet leave tiny indents on the soil and I count them. Three hundred so far since passing the place my eyes first landed on hers. Where her jasmine scent overwhelmed my senses.

I'll make this right between us. I vow it.

Up ahead there's a fork in the road and not much else, but then she whispers something under breath and I'm bombarded by different smells, hers being the most prevalent.

Is this where she and her siblings hid after losing their parents?

They were by themselves, my mate scared and carrying the weight of her grief while I persecuted them from the other side. I've never felt more like a piece of shit than at this moment.

A whimper builds in my throat, my wolf just as devastated.

We could've protected them. Been her refuge.

We move deeper into the property, and I catch a different scent. It's fresher than the others, and male. It's all over the place and I hate it, causes my fur to bristle, and the threatening snarl sits at the top of my snout when she tilts her head.

"You can come out now. I know you've been following me."

A chuffed sound leaves my snout. *Of course, she knew.* I step out from behind a tree and make my way to her, gait slow and my entire being radiating a calm I don't feel. The need to rub myself against her, embed my scent deep into her pores is near maddening—I'll never accept another man near her trying to take what's mine.

And while she glares me down, lips pursed, my beast—king of

all werewolves—wags his tail.

This is what my wolf has always needed, and it came in the package of a five-foot-nothing female with the prettiest eyes and sinful mouth. With thick curves, her hips and arse are perfection while her perky breasts make my mouth water.

But that beauty extends inward, too.

Loyal. Honest.

Currently daring me to test her patience.

"Shift, please."

No real strength behind the command, but I follow it just the same, standing before her in the nude seconds later. My muscles thicken and my cock bobs under her inspection.

"Little Moon, I'm—"

"Why do you keep calling me that?" she cuts me off, her annoyance clear. I don't take offense to it either.

I'm not idiotic enough to believe everything would be forgiven or forgotten in a few short hours. Isabella's processing. I am, too.

And where I'm choking on regret, she's angry.

Hurt.

Overwhelmed.

Exhausted.

Rightfully so, and the last thing I want to do is add frustration to the list, but letting her wander through the woods alone is out of the question. Anyone could attack her in the unclaimed land where rogues and other dangerous creatures reside.

"Because a part of me has always worshipped you." Mere feet separate us but for each step I take forward, she moves one back. "We claimed you before we knew what you were, and even after, it didn't stop us from wanting you. From visiting that lake every night in hopes I'd see you."

"Your wolf has never been the problem."

"I know."

"And I'm not yours."

"You are by the god's design, but I vow to earn the right to your heart."

"Life isn't that simple."

"Nothing worthwhile ever is."

Those words set her off. Tears glisten in her blue eyes, and her face scrunches up in despair. I know I've hurt her, her trust in me, and I'll take it.

All of it. Her.

"I'm not yours," she hisses out, jamming a dainty finger into my chest. Try as she might, Isabella can't ignore my rippling muscles or how my over seven-foot frame contracts at her mere touch. There's also my hard cock and how it throbs against her clothed stomach, a body she's pressing against me. I'm naked, she's not, and it's taking everything in me to not grab her and tear the flimsy fabric from her flesh. "I warned you, Werewolf. Three times we'd meet, and you chose to ignore me. You didn't choose me."

That vow to forget me will never be. I'll follow her in this life and the next and every reincarnation that follows. If holding on to her ire and indignation helps her process and later forgive me, I more than earned the beating, but she'll never erase me from her soul.

"I'm sorry." Two words full of my remorse. "I hate that I've caused you this pain. That we're in this position."

"Why, Xadiel? Why couldn't you just listen to me?"

"Because I blamed myself for not protecting her!" Seconds after my confession, the late-night sky cracks with lightning, the force shaking the ground. A storm's coming; I sense the volatile shift in the air, but neither of us cares. Instead, I crowd her space and pin her against a large hollow tree on her familial lands. "They made us believe she'd been killed, Little Moon. The memory of that decapi-tated body still haunts me, left for us to find as if she were rubbish, and it reminds me that life is short. Everything can be taken—I could lose *you*."

Her emotions are mine, and I know she's feeling my truth. It softens her a bit, just a smidge, but then she bares her tiny Wiccan teeth at me...

19

Isabella

The memory of his office comes to the forefront.

He never gave me his trust. Ignored me.

I push him away, but the beast doesn't budge, further irritating me. "Move."

"I'm not going anywhere."

"Why now? Huh?" Another shove, my nails digging into his flesh. I want to mark him. Make him bleed. "Out of gratitude?"

"You're my mate, Isabella. I know I've—"

"So I'm your mate when it's convenient? Is that it?" His skin breaks and my fingertips become wet, yet he doesn't so much as flinch. If anything, he presses against the edge, wanting me to cut him. Welcoming the sting. "Answer me, Alpha King. I begged you to let me open your eyes. All of this—"

"Is my fault." Low. Contrite. His face contorts and the misery there tugs at my heart, lowering the rage to a simmering thrum. Still there, but now equally exposed and bleeding.

This is the last thing I want for him…for us.

Maybe we should reject the other. End it all.

"Never."

"Excuse me?" The first drop falls and it hits his forehead, rolling down the path to his chin before landing on me. It slides to my bottom lip and my reaction is automatic, licking the droplet and savoring the tiniest hint of his taste. A hum of pure pleasure escapes me, one I can't fight back, while he follows the move with hunger, and the swirl of black enlarges until very little is left of the golden color.

The look in that gaze is possessive while my own need ignites at his close proximity.

His mere presence makes me forget the woman and her knowledge of the stones. I tried to find her before leaving, asked a few scurrying maids who wouldn't meet my gaze about her, but none had seen her. Ever.

That's what I should be focusing on. Protecting my family, but his chest expands and I lose track of my thoughts. His need strikes like a whip against my frail senses, and I whimper without meaning to.

"You spoke out loud." Husky, voice crooning the words while goose bumps rise across my flesh, and it has nothing to do with the slight drop in temperature. Or the light rain drizzling over the treetop and filtering through the leaves. More and more fall, yet I'm flushed. Sensitive.

I'm balancing on a tiny ledge, and either way I tumble will land me in his arms.

This is beyond me. Beyond him.

"I did?" *Gods help me.* The house is a few yards away. So close, and if I could just run...

"Yes." Closer, and I'm sandwiched between the bark and him, each digging into my skin and creating a different reaction. One begs for me to rationalize, to think, while the other wants to let go and accept what will always be. Nothing will ever satisfy me more than *him.*

Breathing harder, I'm no longer pointing, but petting now— stroking his bare chest and enjoying the rumble underneath my palm. This is dangerous for me, but the longer I feel all of him, the lower my inhibitions become.

There's this heat building at the core of me, a clawing underneath my skin that wants to be devoured by him. To let go and for once, take what I want.

No worrying about my family.

Not thinking about keeping them on the right path.

Forgetting what he's put me through.

For once, I want to be selfish. What I want.

My gift of sight comes with a heavy price many don't understand; it takes more than it gives. Seeing the inevitable makes you relive the heartbreak while simultaneously forcing you to accept what cannot be changed.

This is one of those instances I want to fight. To not give in to what we are: two halves of a whole created to give and take while walking this life together. Xadiel Evergreen lives in the very makeup of my DNA—the most precious part of me—and I can't deny the pull.

But then he purrs for me and my mind stops, a ripple effect as I whine for the first time in my life. It's not a noise that witches make, not like this, and he answers my call with a low growl.

I know what he wants. Deep down, I do too.

And the trickle of my arousal further proves that. I'm wet and throbbing between my legs, can feel each drop as it clings to my labia and then falls onto my thighs, thighs I'm currently rubbing together.

"My female." It's a rumble, so deep. An unsatiated yearning. "So fucking beautiful."

"Xadiel, I…" I'm shaking, unable to breathe as his now clawed hand travels from my hip to the underside of my breasts, teasing me over the material of my dress. Just the tip, a gentle back and forth, but it feels so good. "Oh *fuck.*"

"Yes, love?" Another pass, this one across each nipple, and I moan. The sound is loud in the dead of night while the rain picks up. Lighting strikes and the trees sway, absorbing the gift of water while it clings to our skin. His lips don't touch mine, but rather sweep across my cheek to just below my ear where one fang nicks the skin. "Tell me what you need, and I'll move heaven and earth to lay it at your feet."

"We shouldn't." My last attempt, even if it's the last thing I want.

"Tell me to stop, baby. I'll honor your every request." Words don't form and my throat only manages another needy sound, body trembling in his hold. A hold that loosens. Xadiel tries to back up and give me a little space. "Say it. Say *stop.*"

"No."

"Isabella, I'll—"

"Touch me."

"Where, little witch?" The sound of fabric tearing is loud while the sting of it being ripped from my skin makes me hiss. I like the slight sting and the resounding growl that follows as he takes me in.

He's seen most of me, but not like this.

Nature is my playground and surrounded by the trees and rain. I'm free. I'm also his.

"Everywhere, Alpha. Make me yours."

"Motherfuck," he exhales roughly, eyes on my thigh where the tattoo of his wolf takes up most of my upper leg. It's the first time he's seen it. His office was too frantic, and the natural gold bleeds into the black as his human side retakes control. Both are there, but

148

it's Xadiel who reaches down and touches the image with reverence. As if he can't believe it.

Without a word, he's soft and sweet before that same massive hand grips my hip and tugs me forward. Our bodies crash and stumble a bit, but I'm safe with him. Know this like I know my own name. "I don't deserve you, Isabella."

"You've been lost."

"But I should've recognized you for what you are...*my home. My life*." With ease, he lifts me and my legs go around his waist, our lips now hovering. His length is also at my entrance, not entering but kissing the flexing hole. "I'll make it up to you."

"Will you?"

"My life is yours." His nose nuzzles mine. "One taste of you was never enough. So sweet, and all I've wanted was you like this."

"How?" Another low, keening whine. "Please."

"You're mine to cherish and fuck. Do you understand that?"

"I do. So much it hurts."

"Then let me soothe your aches." Then he's kissing me and the world fades away. It's reverent and sweet with just the right touch of desperation to set my heart ablaze. Our tongues twine and teeth click, the sharpness of his fangs heightening the pulse in my clit.

I find them sexy. The knowledge that he can pierce my skin is dangerous and arousing; I want him to. It's why I grip his hair and tug, moving his head to *my* liking in provocation.

Wolves like to be in control.

Alpha want complete submission.

I'm neither. Not yet.

Another sharp yank, and I leave his mouth to lick his Adam's apple. Forcing his head back, I suck hard on the flesh there and the following grunt of approval settles where I'm most sensitive. My breasts ache. Pussy is swollen and waiting.

I'm a virgin, but not prudish.

I know pleasure. Have touched myself many times, but it's his cock that will soothe this burning desire. *I want his knot.*

"You're heaven, Isabella. Made for me." Another growl, and his praise makes me want to drop to my knees and present. To feel the pain and stretch of my first time, but there's another need rising. "Give me your mouth, baby."

"No." With a coy smile, I rake my teeth from his neck to chin and back to his lips. Bite down on his bottom one while his dick presses against my entrance. Rubs back and forth, the swollen head nudging my bundle of nerves with each pass. "And you need to put me down."

Without pause he does, not questioning or complaining, but that changes once I drop to my knees. The sight of me like this causes a feral sound to leave his lips, lips that are curving over his fangs while his chest vibrates.

He's hard and thick, bobbing mere inches from my face while I scent him. My breath caresses the tip while my hands stroke each thigh, sweeping my fingers from his feet to the V of his hips and then back down again. And again. Three times until the bead of pre-come falls, marking the ground.

He's a part of the land. Mine.

Instinct is a beautiful thing and I release control to my nature, taking the head between my lips while my tongue flicks the slit. The pure essence of him explodes on my tongue and I moan, arching my back while my knees widen, exposing my holes to the cool breeze. A sight he devours from above me, standing tall like the beast he is, and nostrils expanding while his hands clench into tight fists.

His claws cut him, tearing flesh open, and blood seeps from the wound. Xadiel never flinches, merely brings one of the bleeding palms to my face and presses it to my cheek. Another mark. Another way to claim me, and I take him deeper into my mouth as a reward.

I know we have a lot to talk about and fix, to work on trust, but I'm a witch and claiming comes with emotion. In his own way, he's always cared for me and that satisfies my nature. I'm preening for him, mouth full of cock, and the man smiles at me.

"You can take more, sweetheart. Let me kiss the back of your throat." I do so with hesitation, relaxing my body the deeper he goes. I'm not an expert, but what I am is turned on by the way he groans— the purr of approval he gifts me—when I'm more than halfway down and stop to swallow. Then again, I hollow my cheeks on the downward stroke and add pressure to the underside with my tongue on the way up. "Good girl."

It's rhythm he approves of. Pumps his hips to.

Slowly at first, Xadiel's testing me and I meet him halfway every time, never giving up control and he doesn't push for it either. It's a process, learning what he likes and how far I can go with his size, but when I pull off this time, I tap his thigh and he stills.

Licking my lips, I look up at him from beneath my lashes. "I want to try something."

"I'm yours to do with as you please."

"Thank you." My body is alight with electrical pinpricks—the bond between us is strong although it's not complete. Yet in this moment, I am so attuned to his every movement and breath, can feel his pleasure as if it were my own. There's also pride a second later when I take him in deep and don't stop until I press my lips to the knot at his base. The bulge is thick and vibrates against my mouth, growing the longer I worship it, but then I'm not.

In one swift move, I'm off his cock and turned around with his body hovering over mine.

Xadiel's mounting me; his wolf is present in the claws gripping the ground and his fangs at the back of my throat. It's feral, and I approve. My body craves this connection on the most basic level, and I give him a nod.

Words escape me. All I can do is feel and let go.

"I'm sorry, my female. I've wronged you, and that's a burden I'll carry for the rest of our lives." His knees force mine further apart while his cock spreads my wetness from entrance to clit and back again. "Please know your hurt is mine. That I will one day earn your forgiveness." The bulbous tip pauses at my hole on the next slide and

ELENA M. REYES

he holds it there. "I will never let you go, Little Moon. No man or beast will cherish you more."

My lips part to respond, but all that leaves me is a scream of rapture when he buries himself to the hilt in one smooth thrust. There's a tinge of pain. I feel split in two, but a rightness accompanies the moment. I take him with no hesitation; I'm built to fit around him like a glove.

Inside me, Xadiel throbs yet remains still. He's pulsing, the low throb relaxing my muscles while the knot at the base rests against the outside of my labia. Not pushing but massaging, and I shake beneath him.

I'm not in pain.

If anything, I want. "Please move."

"Are you sure, sweetheart? I don't want you in pain."

My answer comes in the form of the squeezing walls, pulling him in deeper. "Need more."

"Fuck, you're perfect." One hand retakes its place at my hip while the other lifts, and I look back at him from over my shoulder, catching the moment it comes down sharply on my asscheek. Right then left, and then once again. It stings and warms my skin, but Gods, does it feel good. "You're mine, Little Moon. Death will never do us part."

Xadiel pulls out slowly, dragging his heavy cock against my walls before slamming back in, and he doesn't stop after. I'm ridden fast and hard and without pause. It's heaven and hell converging, crashing into each other and leaving behind a mess of useless limbs.

I can't do anything but dig my fingertips into the dirt, ripping grass, and hold on while he controls me. My body and mind are his. He's all I feel and see and understand. "Xadiel, I'm close."

A whisper he responds to with a hum. Satisfaction drips from the sound, but that's not enough for him and I'm raised higher by his hold on my hips. My hands brace on the ground, trying to find purchase, as Xadiel forces me off and on his cock. Bouncing me at an angle that shatters me while his claws cut my skin.

"Fuck, baby girl. Just like that." Another brutal thrust. His tongue licks my shoulder. "I can feel your walls tightening...love the way your wetness drips down my cock."

"Xadiel, please. *Please.*" This sensation is new and overwhelming, almost painful, but his purring re-centers me. It's what I focus on as the pleasure mounts, riding me high. What I'm clinging to as his knot nudges my entrance, stretching me wide while his lips are on my neck.

He loves the skin with warm, open-mouthed kisses. My bite isn't healed there, but it's better thanks to him. It's scabbing over since I haven't accepted him *yet*, but the attention still sets me off. Blindsides me with its sensitivity.

The orgasm rips through my body with blinding speed; I lose myself to the bliss coursing through my veins. Nothing could be better than this. Being with him is...

"Goddess, Alpha."

"Take it, Little Moon. This knot is yours." Xadiel's gritted words are accompanied by a single punch of his hips, forcing me to take the last bit of him inside. His bulge slips past my slick lips, stretching me tightly around the girth before it swells and locks. We can't move, but the vibration his cock emits as he comes is otherworldly.

Each spurt of his seed pulls a miniature orgasm from me. I'm filled to the brim, but there's still more, and all I can do is lay beneath him and close my eyes. Exhaustion settles deep within me; I'm a mess and sated. My upper thighs are wet and the scent of sex surrounds us.

And the longer we stay like this, being rocked with his knot inside me, the heavier my lids become. Slowly they close and my breathing evens, but Xadiel continues to give me short little jabs that prologue this blissful state that I succumb to.

"You're mine, Isabella. Today, tomorrow, and always."

20
Isabella

I awake to the running of his fingers on my thigh. It's a slow sweep, back and forth and sometimes tracing the tattoo of his wolf.

There's awe in him over it. He's proud.

But the emotion that comes across the strongest is affection. Clear, true, and honest, which leaves me breathless and with new doubts.

This isn't something that happened yesterday. His aura is sweet and melds with mine. Our tethers match. The wolf in him has never denounced me, but the man held back. Felt the same but chose to turn his back on the bond because of a lie.

This was beyond us. But more importantly, can I honestly blame him?

If his family were responsible for Mom and Dad's death, would I react the same?

A difficult answer: I was never put in his position. A rationalization that helps soothe most of my lingering hurt.

It's not his fault. Greed is a horrible thing and is at play here, once again trying to take from me all that I love.

Because I do. For twelve months I've known about him, dreamt of him, and now that I've felt him…Xadiel Evergreen completes me.

"I can feel your eyes on me, mate," Xadiel says, pulling me from my thoughts. His smile is roguish, golden orbs holding nothing but warmth when they finally flick to mine. "Did you sleep okay? Are you sore?"

"Not sure yet." I'm teasing him, but he doesn't catch on and his brows furrow. "I'm fine, Alpha."

"For your first time, I was rough. Should've taken it—"

"It was perfect, and I don't regret a thing. Even slept next to the equivalent of a roaring fire last night." For a second, warmth floods his cheeks and I find the act sweet—special—knowing he wouldn't do this in front of anyone else.

That smile is mine. I know this.

"I'm glad I could help you. It was my first time, too, and—"

"Wait. What?" He can't be serious.

"Does it surprise you?"

"It does." Raising my head from the bed, I pause and take notice of our arrangement. We're naked and lying on a bed inside my family's home; his head is currently using my stomach as a pillow. How he got us inside or knew this space was mine? I have no clue, but thank the Gods he didn't use anyone else's room to crash.

We're also no longer connected, something that makes me blush

—the memory of his knot causing goose bumps to rise across my skin.

"Why?" The amusement in his tone causes me to meet his stare. Almost as if he knows where my thoughts drifted to. "Tell me what surprises you?"

"Well, to start off..." I lick my bottom lip, a little nervousness settling in. He picks up on this and gives my thigh a squeeze, a low purr greeting me a second later. "That's not fair."

"Not meant to be." Admits this with no shame. "One of my jobs as your mate is to bring you comfort, Little Moon. My call was made to resonate only with you."

"Is it crazy that I kind of like that?"

"Not at all." Turning his face into my abdomen, he bites me. Just a quick nip. "It pleases me greatly to take care of you in any way. Just like the tattoo on your thigh is an honor. It's beautiful."

"Thank you. I've had it for quite some time."

"How long?"

I blush. "A year."

"How? If you don't mind me asking." Another soft caress across the marking, and I shiver. Hiding my reactions to him are nearly impossible. Just can't.

"It came after a dream. My first of you." Licking my lips, I look away and pretend to be searching for something. He's guilt-ridden enough and doesn't need the details of that painful experience or the recent one. "I've had many with you."

"I like that you do and have, won't deny it. It's sexy." Playfully, he snaps his teeth at me. "Now, ask me whatever you need to."

"How old are you?"

His laughter booms, shaking my entire body and bed frame. "That's what you're nervous about? You're absolutely adorable."

"That's not an answer, Alpha King."

His amusement dies at once. "Please don't call me that. I don't want titles between us."

"Even when I ask you for my mating bite?" My grin is coy and I know I'm blushing, but he needs to know I'm not trying to push him away by using it. "It might not be tomorrow...I need time, but *someday.*"

"Yeah?"

"Yeah." No sooner has the word slipped past my lips, than we're face to face. His naked body is over mine with a hard cock between us. "Hi."

"So pretty." Xadiel lowers his mouth and pecks me gently. Once, twice...four times. "The day you do, I'll be both honored and harder than steel. Elated and thanking the goddess because I didn't lose you."

"You didn't." The truth. One he deserves to know. "I just need to process and forget."

"I'll wait." I find no annoyance or deceit in his eyes.

"Thank you."

"Never thank me for giving you what you need, even if it's time. Okay?"

"Yes, sir."

"Cheeky. I like it."

A giggle slips from me. "Dork."

"No. I'm a ninety-year-old werewolf who found his mate and wants to lay the world at her dainty feet." He looks down at the scabbed-over bite mark with longing. I feel his regret. "I'm a man who's never touched another woman because I knew it'd hurt my female. Because she'd be worth waiting for, and you're more than special, Isabella. You're everything."

Two days later we're back on Italian soil, and this time I'm traveling with more than one guard. I'm atop Pearl, the Salernitano horse, who's neighing softly. She's a little tense, while wolves

157

surround us on all sides. At the front is Xadiel in his other form, ears flicked back and gaze taking in our surroundings, but he's attuned to me.

If I sigh or shift or so much as breathe in a way that shows signs of discomfort, he makes us stop.

He's proven it to me a few times now, going as far as to try and forbid me from opening the portal that allowed us to cross from his forest to mine without endless days of travel. Right now, I'm not afraid of being caught. Not with his protection and that of the guards.

His order didn't work, but I gave him points for the effort and show of care.

I need to tell him about the fae woman. Maybe he can help me without asking too many questions. Not because he shouldn't, but because my trust in him isn't strong enough to confide something so crucial about me and my sister.

What if he turns me away? Or worse, doesn't believe me?

Our relationship right now is tentative at best, and I need more than one night to open up.

Cain makes a noise and I snap back to the present, forcing myself to lay it to rest for the time being. He's to my right while another soldier takes the left, and five more make up the rear. I was introduced to them as their Queen Luna while they all kneeled, of their own volition, and tapped their chests with a closed fist. The act reminded me of the Wiccan military and the vows they take before being allowed to serve.

To protect. To respect. To defend those weak and defenseless.

"I know, Pearl. We're almost there." I'm beginning to feel the edge of our protection spell. It reaches out and recognizes—welcomes me like an old friend—while still being cautious of the others with me. My calmness, though, helps lower the wards, and we pass through the border without any problems. "Onyx should be back by now, too. Eating and running free...waiting on you."

Pearl gives a little trot at that, happy. She also shows me her teeth in a smile.

"You ready for your bucket of carrots?" I ask her and look up, shrugging when I catch every shifter looking at me. These horses are important to my family. "Get used to it. They're spoiled."

Xadiel chuffs up ahead, the equivalent to a snort, but then he stops. Immediately, his fur bristles and a low growl reverberates through the silent woods. It's too silent, and I smile.

"Come out, Augusto. It's safe."

Our loyal guard steps out from my right and his eyes settle on mine. He ignores the wolves' threatening stance, his posture lax, and gives me a nod. "By blood and pact..."

"We are one."

One by one, the others with him step forward, lowering their weapons before dropping to one knee. They bow in greeting while my mate shifts, walking toward my horse that carries his extra clothing. The others will be provided for with what we have, but he didn't think we'd have anything here that would fit his large stature and build.

Xadiel grabs the change of clothes and slips the trousers on before the undershirt, sans underwear. Next are his shoes, a pair of black boots with the laces undone. He's silent the entire time, watching the guards, but he's satisfied after a while and I'm proud to watch him reach out a hand toward Augusto first.

"King Xadiel Evergreen, Isabella's mate."

Augusto's eyes widen as do several others while accepting the offered. He knew my mate was there, just not whom he was, and much less someone who's hated our kind for so long. "A pleasure, your highness. I'm—"

"Isa!" a voice yells out, his footsteps rushing my way, and I'm off my horse before Xadiel can help me. I land on the balls of my feet seconds before a body crashes into me, the scent of rain and citrus wrapping around me in a tight hug. This is the longest we've gone without seeing each other, my caring for him, and I've missed the kid something fierce. "You're back."

"I'm here, my king."

"Already?" he whines in the way only a teenager can, and those around us laugh. He's still a little shy around strangers, more so after the attack, but I'm humbled again when Xadiel approaches where we stand slowly. His smile is small, holding in his hand something I can't quite make out. "Who's that?"

"My kind-of mate." My whisper matches his.

"For real?" Leo looks at him again, from head to toe. And I'm doing the same to him, looking for any bruises or signs of distress—I wasn't lying to Roberto. One mark on my brother, and I'd kill him. "He's huge."

"You'll grow into the role, too, young king," Xadiel interjects while holding out his gift. It's wrapped in a fine silk, and Leo quickly takes it and unwraps it like the kid he is. The object is a beautiful dagger with an opal-stoned hilt, shiny and blessed, the silver blade glinting in the midday sun.

"This is so cool. Thank you, almost-mate-of-Isabella." My brother can't stop looking at the knife with wonder. "It feels different, too. Like something's calling to me."

"What do you mean?" I share a look with Xadiel. "A voice or...?"

"Like family." Leo nods to himself. "Yeah, like someone very important wants to say hello."

"Why don't you go ahead and put that away in the house. I'll be right behind...you."

"He's fast and enthusiastic." We're watching my excited brother rush away, waving the dagger in his hand like a prize of war and not a gift. "Reminds me of myself at that age."

"Very." Leo's reaction worries me. *What could possibly be trying to communicate?*

"...and he isn't telepathic or empathetic?"

"His powers haven't presented themselves yet. Not that I'm aware of." I need to speak with Uncle Roberto. "We haven't been separated that long to—"

"I used that knife to torture Bartolo, Isabella. It's fae essence he feels."

"Why give him that? What do the fae have—?" I'm cut off and see it. *Leo grown up and standing beside a beautiful woman, her smile radiant and aura sweet and calm, a perfect balance to my brother's strong will. They're staring at each other, the word mate slipping past his lips when another man enters the room and swings his sword at her.*

"Little Moon?" Xadiel calls out, his hand shaking me lightly. "Are you okay?"

"Yeah. Just saw something."

"Bad?"

"Not sure yet, but that knife is only the beginning."

———

WE'RE INSIDE THE FAMILY MAUSOLEUM AFTER THE CEREMONY. People are rushing around outside, the chanting still high and loud while our people celebrate the lives of their fallen king and queen. It was hard on Gabby, on all of us, to release their souls and send them off to the afterlife, but part of life is accepting death.

We are born to die. It's the circle of life.

Our mates and family have each gone their separate ways for now while the rest of the coven sings. Uncle Roberto is avoiding me, while Theodore and Xadiel are tolerating each other; vampires and werewolves have found a common ground, and it's because of us. Neither wants to hurt their mate, in my case more than mine has, and understand how sacred the bonds are.

By blood and pact, we are one.

One soul. One heart. One people.

"How are you really, Isa?" Gabriella asks from her seat beside Mom's urn. It's silent in here, nothing like the swirl of air—the heavy scent of lavender and patchouli that greeted us earlier. Now it's a light remembrance. Their souls have been let go, while this place keeps a tiny piece of their essence for us to visit. The private building on the property is for family only, where we come to spend time and reflect, but right now my twin watches me with knowing eyes.

Our connection has always been strong.

It's hard for us to keep anything from the other, but I've had to. Hurts to do so.

I can't lose either of them. I'll do whatever must be done to ensure their happiness.

"I'm hanging in there, Sister. It's the best answer I can give you, to be honest."

"I can see that."

"Go ahead and ask." Wiping Dad's urn, I place him inside the opened stone door and hold a hand out. Gabriella picks up Mom's and kisses the top before handing that one over as well. Side by side, they'll rest inside the deep box at the center of this wall.

Just like in real life. Always together.

"What happened to you, Isa? You're happy, but there's this heaviness in your bones—a tear in your heart that I see clear as day."

"I'm just exhausted."

"The truth this time."

For a second, I'm angry at her for the interrogation. For seeing the scars I wish remained hidden, but those green eyes full of unshed tears break me. And I cry. Crumble to the floor and release a year's worth of pain and falls and the freaking bond that won't let me rest.

One second, I want to hate him, and the next, beg him to never let me go.

But life is cruel, and nothing is ever guaranteed. I love a man who almost killed me without knowing; a witch after rejection loses her sanity.

"Let it out. I got you." Her arms wrap around me while the glow of candlelight bathes us in warmth. The four walls offer protection.

"He almost rejected me, Gabby. How do I forget that?"

"You don't." My eyes snap to hers through blurry ones. Her

small fingers wipe under my eyes, her expression soft. "You fight and show him that a world without you in it, isn't worth living. You forgive because life is short, and being happy is better than being miserable. And lastly, you'll kick his huge arse when he forgets those two things."

I snort at the last one. "Really? Arse?"

"He's British." She shrugs. "It's fitting."

"True." For a beat we're quiet, but I'm the first to break the silence. "The accent is sexy. Especially in that deep baritone of his."

"Don't tell Theo, but I agree. Although, Italians give them a run for their money."

"So true."

Then we're laughing and Gods, I needed that. I'm giggling while she tries to fight it back, but when one stops, the other begins, and it's a vicious cycle.

My stomach hurts by the end, and she's wiping her eyes. We're loud, I know, and it takes a knock on the door for us to stop. We should feel contrite, but don't. Especially with how light the room feels now. As if cleansed. Our parents are happy, too.

Their small lingering essences almost smile.

Another knock, a bit impatient now, and we stand up from the floor, dusting ourselves off.

Two scents await us. Two grumbly kings.

"*Te amo. Invenire in pace.*" Gabriella and I say in unison, touching our lips to the stone before walking toward the entrance hand in hand. She opens the door and steps outside first, greeting her mate who's quick to pick her up and leave.

Xadiel is also there, and he's looking at me with worried eyes, taking me in from head to toe. "Are you okay, Isabella? I felt the rapid shifts in your emotions and ran over."

Nothing he could've said would be more perfect than that right now. In a moment where I felt alone and unseen, he came because I was sad. Because he's worried.

That's caring. That's being a good mate.

It's why I don't think, and with a hand on his shirt, I pull him down to my level and press my lips to his. The kiss is short and sweet and a promise.

I will fight and forgive and love him.

We will all be okay. I'm starting to truly believe that.

21
ALPHA
XADIEL

I've been away from my lands for a few days now while my female visited with her family and friends. I've let my father handle the pack duties and pushed aside meeting with other leaders while I stood beside her as she wept and celebrated. I watched as she and her siblings laid her parents to rest in a beautiful ceremony that gave me a peek into who they are as a people.

They're not much different than wolves.

We love and bleed the same. We mourn and cry and lose a part of ourselves when someone we care about passes on to the next life.

Life is an individual journey with no regard for emotions or attachments; our expiration is inevitable. Our purposes are different. But that doesn't mean we don't touch the lives of many during our time here, and that comes with a price.

Love is pain; a beautiful destruction worth every moment of anguish when it's lost.

I felt humbled in their presence. My guards did too.

We were embarrassed by how we've viewed and treated witches in the past.

But never again. My allegiance to them is cemented in stone, written in the book of life and signed by my blood. Isabella is mine, and that includes every part of her: physically, family, and responsibilities—her people. They all have my protection and that of the werewolves until the end of time.

"Where are we going, Xadiel?" Isabella asks from beside me, her tiny strides forcing me to slow down considerably. To any outsider, this must look ridiculous. Three of hers are the equivalent to one of mine, but I wouldn't have it any other way.

It's adorable how she power walks, her cheeks flushed pink, but is still slow. More so when her eyes try to take in everything in our house. Years of artifacts and old paintings and the occasional book; Isabella asks about each one, and I'm only too happy to explain what they are or represent.

She loves the history. Soaks up anything to do with our traditions.

I'm thankful she agreed to come home with me and not stay back in Italy.

"It's a surprise, Little Moon. Patience."

"Seers are not patient, Werewolf. We *literally* see the future."

"Sassy, too?" I can't help myself and smack her round left arsecheek, the sound reverberating throughout the quiet room. "That's something I'll quite enjoy, Isabella. Keep it up."

Pink blooms across her cheeks, and she looks away while I bite back a chuckle. Right now, we're heading to the family library where I had a small addition made during our time away. The manor has two libraries: one open to all wolves, and the other is meant for the royals, which is upstairs on the second floor. It's off the landing, the large double doors accessible through a lock system that few know about. It's a puzzle arrangement at the center of the left panel. A seamless jigsaw piece you move to the lower middle and then push inward, the audible click releasing the lock.

Her face is priceless when I look over, her pretty mouth making an '*O*' in surprise. "That was very cool."

"It is." Pulling the handle, I make a path for her to pass and step aside. The space isn't very wide. "After you."

"How chivalrous."

"I try my best." Isabella rolls her eyes but moves to squeeze by, and I click my teeth at her when she does. This makes her squeal, then laugh, and I find the sound to be glorious. Fills my beast and heart with happiness. "Jumpy little thing, aren't you."

"I'm going to get you back for that, Alpha." When she uses the title now, it's playful and so is the glint in her eyes. Nothing like the cold indifference of a few days ago. "Watch your back."

I also find this teasing arousing, and my cock jerks behind the zipper of my trousers, pressing hard against the metal teeth. Then again, I find everything she does a sinful taunt. "Are you, now?"

"Yes." Coy, she looks at me from under her lashes and bites her plump bottom lip. "I am."

"Will you bite me?"

"No."

"No?"

"Yes." At this, I'm confused and give her a surprised look. She reaches a hand out to pat my arm, and I never saw it coming. Isabella shocks me and then laughs. The sharp sting hurts—makes me jump. *How the fuck?*

There's nothing between her fingers. But then she does it again to show me. It's her. As if a live current travels through her. She tries a third time and I attack, pinning her arms down and bite her chin, then bottom lip. I take that sassy mouth hard and fast, killing any rebuttal, and when I step back, she's dazed and smiling.

"I should shock you more often. You get a ten for that kiss."

"You little—"

"That spell is like beginners 101, Werewolf. Baby witches know it; you should be more alert and know these things as a king."

"You're pushing it, Little Moon."

"Then spank me." But before I can reply, she's inside the room and gasps. For a second, I forget our playful banter, worried something is wrong, but calm at the look of total wonder on her face. Isabella stands in the middle of the room with her eyes bouncing back and forth, taking everything in.

Books. Art. Artifacts. Weapons.

She enjoys and appreciates these things. I took notice of this back in Italy—her bedroom, to be precise. There were stacks upon stacks of literature: some academic and pertaining to her species, while others were in Latin and on mythology, which piqued my own interest.

Another pile, the largest, was of romance novels.

Each wall was full to the brim of artwork. Unique pieces and some I didn't understand, but they mean something to her.

"This room has belonged to the Evergreen royals for generations," I say, voice low as I step in behind her and wrap an arm around her waist. One tug and she's against me, no space between us while I lower my mouth to her ear. "It's yours now. My first mating gift to you."

"Xadiel, I can't—"

"You will." My teeth drop, and I skim the tip of a fang against the almost faded bite. Where my mark will someday go. "I want this to be your safe haven, Isabella. The place where you relax and get lost in *for now* until I've earned the right to be your refuge. I'll wait patiently for you, but for now, let this be an extension of me."

I feel wetness on my arm and twirl her around, panicking over the tears, but I find her smiling. So much happiness reflected in those

watery blue orbs and my wolf purrs, matching her mood. Her play-
fulness and open emotions pleas us greatly. This is how our relationship should've been from the start.

"Thank you." Isabella tries to reach for my lips, but her short
stature doesn't help her. She huff and squints, sizing me up, before
doing the absolute cutest thing; she hops. Literally uses her grip on
my shirt to help her propel upward, and still doesn't reach my mouth.
Instead, she manages to touch the edge of my chin, growling in
annoyance. "I'm going to need you to either bend at the waist whenever we're together or invent something that helps me reach your
height, Xadiel."

"What if I like watching you hop like that?"

"It can be arranged in a better situation, but not for a kiss."
Goddess, the mouth on her. She's quick, and her wit is very arousing.
"I'm not going to spend the rest of my life beside you hoping around
like a bunny, Alpha. Leave the acrobatics for the bedroom."

"Done." But then it hits me. She said rest of her life. "Isabella,
did you mean—"

"I'm not ready for your bite, Xadiel, but I know my place is
beside you. There's no anger in me when it comes to you or our past
anymore, but I ask that you give me and my body a chance to recu-
perate. That's all."

"Take whatever you need. All I ask is that at the end, I'm always
your destination." A knock on the door interrupts us before the scent
of my second surprise hits me. "One second."

"What are you up to?"

I don't respond, but instead pull in the serving cart with our
snack that Cain delivered. From pastries and sweets to small sand-
wiches and clotted cream—there are jams and a few different kinds
of breads made today—topping the metal rolling apparatus. Below
on the second shelf they've placed our plates and cutlery and the
main attraction: the piping hot tea.

I'm giving her the first of many afternoon cuppas she'll have
here.

"Please take a seat, my lady. The table has been prepared near the largest window."

"What the...*oh my*," she whispers the last part to herself. In her awe over the room, Isabella missed the clear setup, a table for two beneath a crystal lamp that I'd asked to be added there. "This is amazing."

She tries to help me, but I pat her butt twice. "It's my pleasure to serve you. Go sit."

"Are you sure?"

"I am." And because I can, I steal a quick kiss. Just a peck. "Go on. I'll be right there."

Dazed and smiling, Isabella follows my direction and sits down in her pretty white dress. A theme I've noticed from her; my girl prefers to wear light colors. It looks good on her, too.

This one is short sleeved and a little capped, the bodice tight and with another high split that seems to be her signature style. I love it. Her. The more I'm in her presence, the more I fall head first at her feet.

She's good and sweet and honest. Loyal and loving with those she keeps in her heart.

The tearful goodbyes at the Moore home showed me that side of her. How she hugged every single woman, holding them tight while whispering in their ears. The men all showed respect, Augusto proving himself worthy of his title as general when he bowed to me and promised to take care of her family. He'd watch over and help teach the next king, help mold him into the man his parents saw he'd be one day.

The saddest moments were with her siblings, though. And although we'll see her sister wed soon, the twins are separated by countries.

They cried and then threatened me and Theodore separately, demanded we make our mates happy or else...

That talk with Gabriella didn't come without a taste of her

powers; I had a lot to make up for, and she's well aware of the fact. Rightfully angry on her sister's behalf.

I place the tableware down first and then the food, organizing everything the way my mum advised last night. We'd arrived late and Isabella had gone straight to bed in the luna's suite, much to my bloody hatred of the room now, but I understood. And being unable to find rest without her, I wandered the house and bumped into my mother sitting and waiting with a drink for the two of us.

Almost as if she'd known I'd be restless.

It's where the idea came from.

"Woo her, my boy. Show that beautiful girl that you care and cannot live without her. That you see her... all of her. Give her a grand gesture that shows you pay attention to the little things and that her needs come before your own."

I took that to heart and also take great pleasure in her giddy grin when I push the pastries closer to her. "You have a sweet tooth, my witch? Is that what I'm picking up on?"

"Maybe?" She shrugs, but the wide smile gives her away. Then, there's the way she grabs one quickly and hums with pleasure the second the flaky crust with a custard filling fills her mouth.

"I'll take that as a yes."

"Shut up."

"Did you just shush a king?"

"Yes." No shame, but plenty of that sparkling sass I enjoy. It shows she's comfortable with me, relaxed, and my wolf is pleased. A purr builds in my chest for her, and I take great pleasure in the instant beading of her nipples—the shuddering breath the sound pulls from her.

Motherfucking exquisite.

"Good. You should do it more often," I say, and add a wink. The pink on her cheeks darkens to a full flush at that. *She's affected by my purr, winking, and height.* "Unless you can't handle the games we play. You might lose control and attack me...I am irresistible."

"Did you just question my ability to control myself?" And

171

bloody fuck, I find the mock outrage endearing. Everything about her is. "I'll have you know that—"

"Yes, I did." Picking up a small smoked salmon sandwich, I pop the entire bite into my mouth. She watches me chew, her eyes on my throat. "Like now. You can't look away."

"I can." Still watching. Licks her lips when I swallow.

"Then pay attention to your food and eat."

"I am." *Little liar.*

"Is that so?"

"Hmmm…what the? Wait!" Now she's aware. In one fell swoop, I push my chair back, pick her up, and settle again with her in my lap. Where she belongs. "You can't just grab me like that."

"Too late. Now open." A mini cake, this one chocolate. I place the piece at her mouth and purr again, hardening beneath her arse when she does as I ask, letting me feed her. Giving my wolf and I what we need: to take care of her. "Good girl."

Isabella swallows and glares. "This is so unfair."

"You have a lifetime to get used to it, Little Moon. My world revolves around yours, and I'll live to see you smile."

22
Isabella

I'm sitting beside Xadiel atop the dais in the dining hall, unsure of what's going on, a week after our date. A surprise I can't quite get over because he saw a need in me and fulfilled it without realizing how much I yearned for it.

Books are my life. An enjoyment that always brings me peace when my mind is chaotic and the mental pictures won't let me rest. The storylines within those pages push my visions out of the fore-front—doesn't eliminate them—but give me enough of a reprieve that I can breathe.

They let me escape from reality and forget for a little while.

That library speaks volumes of his affection toward me. Makes me love him all the more.

I need his bite. To be his.

A truth I've been mulling since my talk with Gabriella and more so after my lovely tea-time brunch with Xadiel. The man who made the grand gesture is sweet and kind, yet brutal when needed. He's faithful to his family, unafraid to share his emotions, and chipping away at my resolve with his ability to read me like no one else can.

Like now. Xadiel's smiling at me while sliding his thumb across my knuckles, giving me the courage that I need to do what must be done. Many are congregated here. Faces I've seen a few times now, and they still won't meet my eyes.

Their shame bothers me. I don't want them to feel this way.

What happened, while unfortunate, isn't their fault. Just like Xadiel, they mourned the loss of their queen and lashed out, believing that by doing so, they'd protect those they love.

And if I'm to be their luna, those boulders of guilt can't continue.

Standing from my seat, I clear my throat and every pack member bares its neck. "Look at me." While I'm not their king, my command is carried as such and all faces snap up. A few of the women cry, their tears tugging at my heart, and I do the only thing I can. Through the small emotional string that connects me to them, I send out love. No ill will. No anger. Just love, my true emotions. "What you feel right now is what's in my heart. Please stop looking away or down or avoiding me at all costs, thinking I abhor any of you, because I don't. My mate is a wolf, my soul is tied to your king, and as such, you belong to me, too. I forgive you."

The automatic relief that spreads throughout the large room makes me smile. It crumbles the weight I've been bogged down by, afraid to address, but now I'm glad I did. There's still some lingering hurt—the trauma was felt on both sides—but it's time to heal.

And I'm more than humbled when they all touch their hearts for me. They're my family now, too.

Yet the sound of a stone door opening cuts the happiness, and I gasp, shocked by the sight of two individuals being pushed into the room from the same hole Luna Eda was kept in.

Theresa and Timoth look horrible, smell of human waste, and I scrunch up my nose.

"Thank you, my luna," Xadiel says from beside me, he too standing now as we face the crowd. "Your heart is a treasure, and our people will forever remember your grace."

The pack members cheer at this, clapping and some even whistling, all but the two who stare daggers at us. Timoth doesn't speak, but the woman beside him can't help herself, spewing her hate at me.

"A witch can never be our queen. The whore is unworthy of the title." Beside me, Xadiel steps forward, his muscles tensing and body ready to attack, but I calm him by grabbing his hand. Her words don't matter to me, but this needs to be handled with care.

"And you are, my dear *sister*?" Eda and James take their place in front of us. While this is a public sentencing, the crime of treason and attempted murder is not one taken lightly by any species, and for them, this is personal on another level.

This is Xadiel's aunt. The past luna's sister.

And someone who was a trusted member of their community.

"It should've been mine all along, Eda. You stole my mate from me." A lie, yet many in the crowd give an angry yip, insulted by the idea. "Our parents set up our marriage, his family agreed, but you showed up and I was cast aside like rubbish."

"Because you're not his fated, Theresa. This was never meant for you."

"Bullshit! We could've been happy together!"

"Silence," their alpha king roars, and the hall quiets. Not even Theresa opens her mouth. "What you did is the highest level of wickedness, Theresa Bancroft. You almost killed your sister, did murder your fated, and nearly cost me my luna. How do you plead?"

"Not guilty."

"And you, Timoth? You face the same charges."

The ex-beta looks haggard and done with the entire charade. He's not happy, still as evil in his stare, but resigned at the same time. "Guilty. I took great pleasure in rising against you useless cunts. I could've led us out of the forest, dominated and castigated humanity, but you chose to stand beside the son of the old weak king and a pathetic witch...*son of a bitch.*"

"Never speak of my family that way. I'm done being merciful." His life's essence dances for me, comes a little closer, and I hold it there without pause. I can't kill the way Gabriella can, but the pain she taught me to inflict is just as dangerous. It feels like death. As if your soul leaves your body, and the tug and dance game reflects against your organs. "We will defeat every single one of you. Your leader will never win."

The next moments happen in a blink. One second, I'm inflicting pain, and the next, I'm behind a savage who holds his aunt by the neck. Timoth is on the floor and coughing, his body slow to stand, but before he can fully get to his feet—James is behind him.

Father and son tighten their grips. One has Timoth's arms, forcing them back until there's a resounding crack reverberating throughout the room, and the other tilts his aunt's neck, exposing her throat. His intention is clear, to rip her apart, but then the woman speaks.

"Would you kill a family member for her? I'm your blood, Xadiel."

Silence fills the room. My blood pumps so hard it fills my ears; a small part of me is afraid to hear this answer. Would he forsake me? Would he cast me aside again?

"I'd kill my own mum if she betrayed me or my mate. Isabella Moore is untouchable." That last crack in my heart heals at the conviction—truth—in those words. It's not an empty platitude meant to calm me, to appease my fears, but the vows of a man who loves and wouldn't let harm come to me ever again.

"As he should."

"Eda? How could you say that?" Theresa asks, her situation

finally dawning on her. There is no escape. No more emotional strings to pull. "We're family."

"And by family you shall die." My wolf grabs her hand with his unoccupied one and yanks, tearing the appendage clean off before tossing her at his mother's feet. "She is your kill. Show no mercy."

"Thank you." Eda wastes no time in tackling the other she-wolf to the ground—who's screaming in pain—straddling her waist and landing the first of many blows. She ruthless in her delivery while James forces Timoth to watch for a few seconds, thirty at the most, before ripping the scum's head clean off and tossing it aside.

The wolves here stomp their feet, many shifting and growling as revenge and the blood of an enemy is spilled, yet I'm struck by a different sight. Xadiel kneels at my feet with her hand, ligaments and torn muscle showing, and neck bared. This is the ultimate sign of respect.

A king bending the knee for his female. Showing his pack that I am revered.

Tears spring to my eyes and all else fades away. I don't care about Theresa's screams or the howls from those watching; I drop my mine and cup his face. This act means more to me than words ever could.

He chose me.

"I love you, my alpha king. Always have."

A shuddering breath escapes him, teasing my lips. "And I love you, Little Moon. More than anything in this world."

"Good." My grin is cheeky and eyes mist over, but the way he's looking at me, it's as if he's never seen anything more beautiful. "Because I've been waiting for you to catch up."

"Is that right, love?"

"Yes." A truth I now see. All along, this is what I've needed. *He's truly mine.*

"And what happens when I do?"

"You give me your mating bite, Xadiel Evergreen. Claim me, Alpha."

23
ALPHA
XADIEL

No words have ever been sweeter.

She accepts me. Forgives me.

My chest expands on a rough breath as I watch her from behind the tree line. She's beautiful—a motherfucking goddess, but more importantly, she's a gift. And even while angry, hurt by my own idiocy, her soul never stopped calling out to me. Those soft, sweet tethers greet me with a hum now, almost swaying in pleasure at my mere presence, and my chest vibrates with a purr.

Undeserving as I've been, I let them fall across my bare flesh like a caress while my cock throbs. Drops of pre-come fall to the ground beneath my bare feet, and I pump my length twice while she continues to bathe.

We're far from the manor and alone; I swept her away seconds after the declaration. Between howls and clapping, I acknowledged the pack members with a nod while Mother mind linked me.

Go on, son. Get out of here and claim your beloved.

That was thirty minutes ago and fifteen since I walked away at her request. She wants to relive our dream. To be chased and captured.

And I love her all the more for it. For appeasing the need of my beast.

We will forever treasure this moment.

The water sways around her, that same light from the first time lapping at her upper thighs and arse while she stands near the center. Wind sweeps through the trees and across the water, pushing her red hair aside and exposing that slender neck.

My mating spot is exposed, and my fangs drop. A faint mark is still there, but today's declaration will override it and a new one will appear. The sign of a man and wolf's ownership.

But not yet. I want her to find me first.

A rustle to the left catches her off guard and I bite back a smirk, watching the surprise flash across her features when she realizes it isn't me. Instead, it's a small deer with a piece of the shirt I'd worn earlier today in its mouth, chewing it.

Animals are curious creatures by nature, and this doe scented the predator. By her actions, I guess she felt confident and claimed her prize after not being attacked. Done on purpose and worked to my advantage.

"The hell?" She swims toward the shore, nose twitching. Little Moon knows I'm here, her senses are telling her as much, but she doesn't see me. Until another breeze sweeps through us and those blue orbs find me in the brush.

I growl at her in warning when she takes a few steps back in the water, creating distance between us. As if that would stop me.

I want her pinned beneath me. To taste her tears of pleasure.

Crying out to her wolf for a moment of rest that I'll deny while wringing another orgasm from her.

"Come to me, my female." Loud, the timbre of my words carry through the forest as I step toward her. My footfalls are quiet right now, my beast restless yet awaiting his turn.

"No." One word, and it makes my cock throb. My knot expands.

"Then run, little witch. This is the only chance you'll get." No sooner have the words slipped past my lips than she takes off. Dripping wet and naked, her lithe form is fast—embracing our game of chase—and I pause to inhale deeply.

I let her get ahead of me; I want my prey nervous and slick. Swollen and wanting.

Isabella's heading east, but that doesn't mean she'll stay on that track. Yet I follow her anyway, my pace calm while the wolf comes forth in a half-shift, my clawed feet digging into the ground below. I'm scenting the surroundings, tracking each leaf and tree she's touched in her haste to flee.

No hurry. Just languid steps deeper into the woods while little red runs from her wolf.

Up ahead, I find footprints on the ground and smirk, licking my fangs. The witch is clever, I'll give her that—and the confusion tactics get points for creativity.

In a circle, she's run around a grouping of sequoias that I recognize from our dream. Same one where I kissed and touched—but the indent near a grouping of leaves shows a different direction. Isabella's heading north now and toward open land where she knows danger could lurk.

She's taunting me. Testing to see if I'll protect what's mine.

"Bad girl." Dropping to all fours, I give full control to my animal. My paws pound the ground, diminishing in minutes the distance between us, while my snout remains high. Her scent is potent, stronger the closer I get—as if she's wet or bleeding—and both options without me are unforgivable.

However, the closer to the border I get, it disappears. Completely gone, but I hear her giggle in the breeze.

My head snaps toward the sound, and I find her blowing me a kiss. My head lowers, lip curling over my teeth, and she runs again. This time the chase is close; I'm on her heels before my witch gets past the last marker she left me.

Nipping. Corralling.

I push her past her limit, enjoying the playful screams she emits when I get too close. How she tries to dodge me, turning fast and using the trees to propel her body in the opposite direction, but nothing could keep me from her.

However, her whine when my wolf tackles her and flips us mid-fall will forever be etched into my mind. This one is different. It's not for the man, but a calling to the wolf—a plea to be marked.

I growl at my mate, nipping her shoulder while taking the brunt of the crash with my body. Always protecting her. She lays panting over our fur, smile wide and cheeks flushed while we inhale her lovely jasmine scent.

Ours.

The singular thought expresses how we feel. The peace and hope she brings.

Slowly, I transform beneath her. Letting her experience the shift with me.

Each crack and change until my arms wrap around her. Her heart is beating fast, body shivering, and it's the excitement coursing through her veins that adds to the heady scent.

I could mount her now.

Fill her to the brim with my seed and keep us locked together for hours so they take hold. Claim my queen on the forest floor as the prize she is, but I know where it will mean more.

To her. To me.

Standing with her still in my hold, I carry my witch back the way we came. She doesn't question what I'm doing, why I've yet to bite her, but understanding dawns once we cross the trees leading to our lake. In the late evening sky, the last rays from the sun dances across the still waters, and I walk us to the center with care.

Isabella's eyes shine for me, the blue near glowing as mine do for her. Both her mates are here, needing her acceptance and the privilege to love her.

Placing her on her feet, I cup water with my hands and wash away the sweat and light dusting of dirt that clings to her limbs. I wet her hair and push back the fiery locks, keeping her face and neck clear for my eyes to feast on. There isn't an inch of her I don't caress or touch, massage until she's pliant in my arms.

She's also needy. Her whimpers and moans make me feel a hundred feet tall, but it's her low *please* that makes me snap. I hoist her up and wrap her thighs around my waist, for a second caressing the tattoo on her thigh before lining up with her slick center.

Her pussy sits above my cock; she's soaked, and it has nothing to do with the water. It slides down my length, coating me in her sweetness. I slide between her folds once, twice…three times and on each, her clit kisses the slit at the end of my girth.

It causes her to shiver and try to gyrate, pull me inside, but I hold still. Need her to hear me.

"I love you, Isabella Moore. I'm forever grateful to the goddess above for the gift of my mate and luna. You are my perfection." Then I'm inside her warmth in one fluid thrust, sinking in deep without pause. Not until my swollen knot presses against her labia, and then I fuck her with short, fast strokes.

Each punch of my hips is harder than the last, and she clenches around me, fingernails digging into my shoulders while I keep a rough pace. The skin breaks there, and the slight sting causes my fangs to drop once again. To itch with the need to be buried in her neck—to mark what's ours—as I bounce her up and down my thick shaft.

And Isabella doesn't miss a single pump, meeting me thrust for thrust. The faster I guide her, forcing her hips to slam down, the

louder she moans for me. She's thrashing in my hold—whimpering
—as the knot slips inside a little more with each upward drive.

Then, there's the way her eyes grow dark at the sight of my elon-
gated teeth.

She wants them, too. Shivers and bares her neck to me.

"Mark me, my wolf. I want to be yours." One of her small hands
grips the hair at the back of my neck, guiding me toward her marking
spot. A spot I kiss, swipe my tongue across, and I love the way she
reacts. Little Moon tightens for me, her pussy clamping down so
tight it's almost impossible to move, but I fuck her through each
clench. "I love you, Xadiel Evergreen. I'm proud to have you as my
mate and king."

"My beautiful female," I whisper reverently, holding her closer
before burying my teeth in her neck. Immediately, she hisses in pain,
which turns to pleasure as I slam inside a final time and my knot
expands within her walls. We're locked together as her orgasm and
mine crash into one another. The feeling is indescribable, a plane of
nirvana no one could comprehend much less bloody explain, yet I
reside inside of it with her.

I experience it all with her. Every spurt of my cock filling her
pussy, the squelching noises and the vibration of her screams turned
needy whimpers, and then lastly, the aftershocks of rapture as I rock
into her slowly.

It's all magnified by her emotions, and the most predominant one
is happiness. Pure, unadulterated happiness.

Pulling my fangs from her flesh, I lick the skin and seal my
essence within her. She will forever carry a little of me inside her, her
scent of jasmine merging with my wood and mint. Every wolf and
creature will scent me on her. They will know she's taken and by a
king.

My mark, when healed, will display the royal crown and the
golden bloodline that runs through my veins, much like the one I
have on my back. Hers will be smaller, more delicate, and with the
added details that are fit for a queen.

It's been that way for every king before me and will continue for the ones that follow. Our pups.

I lean my forehead against hers and inhale her exhale. Watch my mate come for me again, a smaller wave this time as the knot vibrates with my purr. "I'm going to spend the rest of my life, work every single day to be worthy of you, Isabella. To be the mate you deserve. The one who loves and supports all that you do; I will never hinder your growth or stop you, but I ask that you take me wherever you go. Your journey will forever be my home." *You were born to be mine.*

The surprise on her face is sweet when she realizes I can speak with her through the mind link. She's now forever a part of werewolves, our history, and will rule beside me for eternity.

My destiny has always been you, my king. Today and always.

"Until the end of time and beyond, little witch. I will always love you."

24
Isabella

I've been ignoring Gabriella the past few months while reliving the same vision over and over again. The pain inside my chest is too great to contain, my grief near suffocating, while putting on a smile for the world to see.

My werewolf can sense something's off, though, but he doesn't ask. Instead, he respects my visions and lets me come to him without asking questions when the pain's too strong to contain. Like when I finally spoke to him about the fae woman inside his home. His concern and reaction was to be expected, helping me search and ask and interrogate a pair of guards serving a sentence for helping Bartolo, but each time we came up empty.

No one saw her. No trace left behind.

Yet I'm prepared for the day we meet again. I know we will.

Through it all, though, Xadiel's been amazing. He's sweet and understanding, lets me be myself, and my life with him will be one of great satisfaction for many years to come.

However, I still mourn what will be lost.

How do I say goodbye to something I never had? How can I face my sister and kill her joy? The simple answer is that I can't. Both break my heart, tear my soul in two, but it's what must be done.

There's a war on our doorstep. Our enemy has risen and taken his stance; the moves made in the shadows are no longer done in silence, and they get bolder each day. King Larue wants the stones to appease Aries and gain his favor. To destroy all monarchies and crumble societies, and all for power. The greed and feeling of superiority that pushes a person to commit atrocities in the name of victory.

I have a stone, and so does Gabby; two gifts made by the gods above to bless our paths and protect the delicate balance between life and death. A black and azure gemstone: one inside Gabriella's chest, and the other in my head—neither of us asked for this.

To lose and sacrifice, but the choices have been made. Forced upon us before we were born.

Thanatos and Gaia bestowed the gift that our parents died protecting. Believed in.

It's why I've kept away. I cannot show my hand beforehand, even if it kills me to know my sister is upset and thinks I've abandoned her. But nothing could be further from the truth.

Gabriella knows I'm hiding something, avoiding, but for the assurance of her rebirth, I'll do what is needed of me. Will give my blood—my very world—if Thanatos asks it of me, and he will. My sacrifice and promise along with Theodore's will cover the cost.

There will be peace until she returns and the true purpose of the stones is revealed. Because the world thinks it's the power of death and my sight, but it's not. Those two are only the beginning.

Larue will someday get his hands on me and offer me a choice. Just as he did the last time we met.

"You have it, don't you?" he asks Gabriella, his tone less acerbic. Almost saccharine. He's not looking at me, but I feel the pressure of his power. It's like a boulder sitting on my head—crushing me—while my mate and family are oblivious. As if blocked to my emotions. "It's why you're so confident?"

"Have what?" I sense Gabby's confusion. The others, too.

"Ask your sister. She knows." At that moment, he slams into my mind and I blank. I can't move and time slows. "Just know that I'm not the only one interested. Many will come for you both."

My patience is waning, young one. You will come to me of your own volition and comply—behave like the good girl you were raised to be—or be forced to watch them all die. *He's in my head. Voice cocky and amused.* **One by one, I will kill them while you watch. Your sister. Her husband. Your mate. Each one will die because of your selfishness before my son takes you as his bride. By choice or by force, you will become our whore. The clock is ticking, Isabella. Choose wisely.**

"Isa?" Her voice snaps me out of the mental hold and I shake him off.

The act surprises King Larue. Me too, but it also gives me a smidgen of hope.

"Not now, Sister. We must go home." And it's the urgency in my voice, the tremor, that has her nodding as we rush out with our mates following. No one says anything, but Xadiel and Gabriella sense something is wrong.

They didn't question my silence that day, but they will in the future.

My allegiance and hand in marriage to his son. Or Xadiel's death and my imprisonment.

In either equation, he never meant to let Gabriella live. She's a vessel he must destroy to gain access to Thanatos's stone; her power is too uncontrollable to dominate. I can't kill with the closing of a fist like she can and the pain I inflict can be stopped, but I'd give my soul to protect the ones I love.

To win, I need them *all* alive. To protect my future child, *I* must suffer now.

However, his kingdom will pay the price for his choices, and that is a vow I made long ago.

Until a new leader arises, blue blood will paint the streets of France.

"Talk to me, Little Moon? You've been quiet since we left home," Xadiel asks, riding behind me as we trot on Pearl back into Moore land. There's a book I need from my bedroom, a memoir written by my father that's been calling to me for days on end. This one didn't go into any of the vaults, felt wrong to do so the day I cleaned his office, and now it wants my attention.

I tried to ignore it, but that changed last night. He whispered in my dream to come and find it.

His voice startled me at first; I couldn't see him no matter how hard I looked, but the voice was unmistakable. There's something in those pages I need to see and after explaining it to Xadiel, we teleported back to Italy not long ago.

Like the last time, the ward is up, reaching out to me and my wolf, allowing us entry once within the border limits. But that's where the similarities end. Death is all around us, feeding the ground, and I recognize it for what it is.

"Blood magic."

"What did you say?" Xadiel pulls on the reins and Pearl halts, shifting from foot to foot. She, too, senses something's off. "What do you see?"

"I don't see...*I feel it.*" Ignoring his command for the horse to stop, I tap her side and she rushes forward at a speed he's not accustomed to. Pearl doesn't pause until we're at the entrance to our home, and my eyes take in the carnage. Bodies on the ground, cut and bleeding—feeding the enchantment of a powerful wielder.

They're alive, but weak. The sight of our people subjugated like this is enough for a red haze of ire to overtake me.

I'm back to the night our parents were killed and I ran with my siblings to safety.

I'm back to finding Meera and what's left of her coven. They were chained and drained like this while some piece-of-shit warlock abused them.

I'm back to Xadiel's almost rejection because of a selfish woman and a fae practitioner's dark influence under Larue's orders. Because it all tracks back to him. The same stench of decay left behind by blood magic.

"We're in this together, |

Isabella. I fight for you."

"And I love you, my king." Turning my face, I give his lips a quick kiss—pour all my love and appreciation into the singular touch —before ripping myself away. He tries to reach for me, but I'm moving faster than I ever have before.

"Isabella!"

"Prohibere. Sanguis ad vos reverteur." All blood flow stops at the powerful command, and those on the floor gasp a heaving breath. They choke, coughing and groaning, but I don't pause to check on anyone as I return what's been taken. They'll be well soon.

My attention is on the house now, and more importantly, a female's bloodcurdling scream that rends the air a second later. It's familiar and came from beyond the wide-open doors—the following crash is loud.

"Get away from her!" Leo yells out, the sudden lash of pain he's feeling cutting me deep. As is his call for Uncle Roberto, begging them to stop whatever is happening. "Why are you doing this? I thought—"

A slap resounds, flesh meeting flesh, and he's silenced. However, a maniacal laugh filters through, and it's female.

Together, love. I'm with you.

Xadiel's large wolf is beside me, his snout pushing my hand and giving a long lick to the palm. I'm blessed to have him.

Always, my Alpha.

No more words are exchanged as we rush inside, and I've never reacted in such a way. The ire from a few minutes ago is magnified, the thrum of sudden power in my veins—unlike my sight—shakes me to the core, and I meet the fae female's eyes. The same bitch I've been searching for from the Evergreen manor, and this time, she's standing over my brother while Roberto lies unconscious.

Her hand is up with a dagger in its grip, an opal hilt I recognize poised above Leo's chest.

My baby brother. He's a child.

The room shakes and things crash to the ground, mirrors and pictures, but I focus on her. I want her neck sliced open and blood marking this floor. Same way she bled my people. Same way she attempted to do with Leo.

I don't see it coming, but Xadiel does. Somehow, he knows what I need and wraps his arms around me in support. His body fortifies mine—centers me—a second before I flick my eyes toward a large shard of glass and then back to her. The piece moves as if commanded, following my desires, and before the woman can jump back, it slashes her shoulder.

Close, but not enough. I want her jugular.

The next one hits her chin and cuts deep, the skin flayed open to the bone, and her scream makes me smile. So does the fact she dropped the perfect weapon, the knife Xadiel gifted Leo months ago.

"What the fuck?" Eyes wide, she stares at me as the scent of fear grows. "How is this even possible? He said you were the weak one."

"Run." One word. My only warning because the dagger shakes on the ground, rising slowly and I tilt my head, watching how it does the same. This is new, a gift I don't know how to control, but I'm not afraid to embrace it.

Five. Four.

She frantically grabs a pouch from her waist and pours the contents onto the ground.

Three. Two.

A portal opens and she grabs Roberto, starts to drag him closer.

One.

A flashing pain rips through me, right at the chest area, and the silver falls to the ground. This consumes me although I'm uninjured, the sudden bout of sorrow, and I feels as though I've been torn in two where I now kneel.

No! Gods, no!

I want to tell Xadiel to grab the woman, to not let her escape, but nothing comes out past the sob I'm choking on. I'm forced to watch through tears as the woman disappears with my uncle. I hear Leo's scream. He too feels it now. So do those outside who wail, their yells drowning out the breaking of my heart.

"Gabriella." She's dead. I can feel it.

"Isa! The book!" Leo stumbles to me, gripping my face hard while my mate growls lowly. I know he's distressed, not under-standing what's happening, but something about the urgency in my little brother's expression snaps me into focus. "Dad left the book for this."

And it hits me then. He also knew. Carries his own burdens and secrets.

"When?"

Leo nods while wiping my cheeks. "It's what he whispered right before we ran that night. *Someday she'll need the book to save Gabby. Remind her when it happens.*"

"It's in my room. Can you grab it for me?"

"No. That's what started this." His eyes shift to a body on the ground. Our aunt is bleeding from her chest, stabbed, but the low rising lets me know she's alive. Hurt, but still here. "Uncle Roberto grabbed it; he was putting it in his suitcase when they started argu-ing. That's when the lady came, demanding it, and she hurt Aunt Silla."

"Where is it now?"

"Under the lose floorboard in my room. I hid it when they weren't looking."

"Xadiel," I whisper, feeling his rumble in answer against my chest. "I need you to check on my aunt and the others outside."

"Done, my little moon." He lifts us from the ground and turns me, eyeing me from head to toe before giving me a soft and sweet kiss. Speaks against my lips. "Do what you must, my love. No matter the cost, I trust you. Will be here when you're ready to talk."

"Thank you, my king."

"We are one, my witch."

Once my mate's next to Silla and checking her pulse, I turn to Leo. I hold my hand up for him and he meets it, palm to palm, before intertwining our fingers. We're going to need to be a united front for this to work. I'll need him to be there when I crash after and find Xadiel.

"You ready, kid?"

"What are we going to do?"

"I'm going to make a bargain with the god of death in exchange for Gabriela's return, little brother. But more importantly, I know what he'll ask for…a life for a life."

"You can't die, Isa. We need you, too."

"Not me." Another pang tears through me, but I grit my teeth and keep walking toward his room. It's near the back and right where he described with Thanatos's prayer opening, the pages flipping on their own the moment I pick it up. Dad's showing us the way, even in death. "But I'll be giving up my right to having children until our sister's return."

It'll be a hundred years before I meet the little one I dream of every night.

EPILOGUE #1

Isabella

ONE YEAR LATER...

I'm staring out onto the pack grounds, watching as the last arrangements are made by the she-wolves in charge. They're all so happy tonight as the moon sits high in the sky. Their emotions wrap me in love as I try to shake off the sadness in my heart.

My family won't be here today. Not even Leo as he's off training with Augusto to help control his awakening powers. Right now, they're volatile—need containment—and there's no one better to help him than the elder guard.

Moreover, I miss them. My father and mother and their warmth; the cocoon of their tethers calming my nerves while cracking jokes. My sister's laughter and at-times-bossy disposition while Leo complains about being hungry.

When will the path of tears end?

"They'd be so proud of you, Isa," a female voice says from behind me and I turn, finding Xadiel's mother dressed in a beautiful velvet gown the same green color as their crest. Her eyes are glossy and her smile soft. "You're a wonderful daughter, a pure soul, and the best gift my son could've been given. I'm so proud to have you in my family, sweetheart. Thank you for giving him a second chance."

"I love him." No answer could be truer than that. "Xadiel is my heart."

"And you are his." Closing the distance between us, she embraces me. Not the first time she's done this, but today, it feels different. Lavender and patchouli, the familiar scent teases my nose, and I swallow hard. *I love you both, too. So much.* "Just as we all knew you'd be mates when you were young."

At that, I pull away just enough to raise a brow, my lips curling into a grin. "How so?"

"When you were but a babe, your mother would bring you girls here. We'd chat and gossip and while Gabriella would play with her dolls, you'd press that adorable face of yours against the window and watch him train." A flush of heat runs through me at that. I'm blushing, but Eda doesn't mention it. Instead, she walks me over to a small couch and we sit, my hand in one of hers. "Isabella, you were awestruck. Would watch him quietly for hours on end while my son would wave here and there. And we'd know the moment he did, because at two-years-old, you'd squeal and clap."

"Why hasn't he ever mentioned this?" I ask, a small giggle slipping from me.

"Because we decided to cloak his memories until you came of age. Neither of you were supposed to know then about the other, and fate took care of that." Eda's grin matches mine as she bumps my shoulder with hers. She's amused. "Your father saw this; it came to him in a vision while they sparred." I'm thrown by that, but brought back into focus by her laughter. Literal peals of laughter, and I'm close to following. No part of me is mad that they hid our connection; I'd be a hypocrite to do so when I carry so much to save so many. "Xadiel nearly knocked Paolo out with a single blow to the temple, while your father tried to make sense of the timelines. Literally beat up by his son-in-law, and my husband never let him forget it."

"Is that why we stopped visiting?" My memories of this place are distant and blurry; I was too young to catalog the details. "Why they kept me and Gabriella isolated? They knew who—"

"Your parents knew they'd die to save you, hours after Leonora gave birth." I gasp, and my chest caves in at the confession. "You two were their little miracles, Isa. They loved you beyond words and knew the sacrifice each of you would make. Just like I've been instructed, and accept happily, to step in and be your shoulder to lean on when the time comes. I might not be your birth mother, sweet girl, but I'm just as proud of you, if not more."

"Eda, I—"

"The world doesn't see your burden, but I know the weight is crushing." I'm not sure when a few tears fall, but she wipes them away a second before the door is thrown open. My beast stands in the doorway, broad chest heaving while our eyes meet. "Keep moving forward. You're his world."

"Thank you."

"When you're ready, call me Mom." Bending over, she kisses my cheek. Her words are spoken low, so only I hear. "I've always seen you as mine."

With that, she gets up and leaves while my mate enters the room. Xadiel walks up to me, his strides powerful and determined. "Talk to me, Little Moon. Your emotions are going from one extreme to the other, and I hate to see you like this. If you want to postpone the luna ceremony until—"

"I'm ready."

"Are you sure?" he asks, tugging me up and then encircling me in his arms before lifting. Nose to nose. Lips hovering. "We can wait until Gabriella returns."

"Are you getting cold paws, my king?" My own hands pet him while smiling, fingers running from his shoulder blades to collarbones, then back again. I'm admiring the muscles there. Loving how strong he is. "Need time to think—"

I'm silenced by a sharp nip to my bottom lip. "Never."

"Then let's get semi-hitched."

His amusement is clear, eyes crinkling at bit at the corners. "Semi?"

"I want a full wedding when she's back, Alpha. I need my family there for me."

"Then so it shall be."

"Thank you."

"Never thank me for taking care of what is mine." Adjusting his grip, I'm shifted, and then kissed. This one is long and sweet, all his love for me pouring into every swipe of his tongue and the sting of his canines. They've dropped, and I lick the right one and then left, giggling when he shivers. "Bad girl." His voice is husky, his intent clear, but then we both hear Eda and he groans.

Xadiel, we're ready. Don't make me come get you.

"Later?"

His smirk is dangerous as is his scent. Headier. "It's a date."

With that, I'm carried out onto the open field where our people are waiting. Many are in wolf form, bowing their heads as we pass. His father and mother are standing at the front, the full moon gracing us with her love while I take my place beside his on the raised platform.

An older wolf greets us, baring his neck while sharing words with the crowd. I pay no mind to him, not when my mate's wolf comes forward and the swirl of black becomes more pronounced. His soul—the beast—is calling to me, and I drop to my knees before him.

I'm offering him my loyalty and love as he did for me a year ago.

I'm offering my blood as signature to our union.

My wolf purrs at the symbolism and he meets me on the dais floor. Even like this, he's so much bigger than I am, but to him we're equals. I'm just as important, and he respects my thoughts—my need for privacy. My alpha accepts me as I am.

I love you with every fiber of my being, my wolf.

He smiles for me then. The one only meant for me.

As I love you, Little Moon.

I don't notice when the blessed blade slides across my hand or the moment he cuts his, but when our palms press together, I'm blanketed by his love. If I thought our connection was strong after his bite and I accepted him as mine; I was wrong. This, our blood intertwining, is everything because Xadiel's looking at me with understanding—a renewed possessiveness that sends shivers down my spine and makes wetness pool between my thighs.

"I remember you, Isabella. I remember my promise to your father."

EPILOGUE #2
XADIEL

A HUNDRED YEARS LATER...

My Dearest Werewolf,

If you're reading this, I am gone and it will be some time before we're reunited.

Please trust in me that I'll return to you, that my love for you knows no bounds, and I will move heaven and earth to always make it so. King Larue is after me. The threats have risen in the last few months, and I accept it's my turn to sacrifice.

There is no other choice for us. Not if our future is to be bright.

You are my heart, Xadiel.

My reason for getting up each morning, and so is our future pup. I've seen him many times, my love. He will be strong, a warrior like you, but to save him I must first play a role.

Yours always,
Little Moon.

HALF TRUTHS: NOW

Isabella

I've lied to those I love the most.
I'm the keeper of all secrets, but I've broken that trust. I don't know if
they'll ever forgive me, but what I've done, I've done out of love and
loyalty.
To my family. To my mate.
To the little one, I dream of every night . . .

Xadiel

Everyone has secrets.
Some are harder to hide than others, and yet, I see the strain in her
eyes. I feel the hopelessness in her soul but have kept my promise to
let fate run its course. Even when the animal within demands to take
control—to fight and be her protector—when it's against herself she
needs saving from.
But then she disappears. Is taken.
I'M A BEAST.
UNTAMED.
WILD.
And I'm coming for what's mine.

FATE'S BITE SERIES
LITTLE LIES
LITTLE MATE
HALF TRUTHS: THEN
HALF TRUTHS: NOW
OMISSION
MEERA AND TERO {TBD}
MARCIA & ALPHA SNAKE {TBD}

ABOUT THE AUTHOR

Elena M. Reyes was born and raised in Miami, Florida. She is the epitome of a Floridian and if she could live in her beloved flip-flops, she would.

As a small child, she was always intrigued with all forms of art—whether it was dancing to island rhythms, or painting with any medium she could get her hands on. Her first taste of writing came to her during her fifth-grade year when her class was prompted to participate in the D. A. R. E. Program and write an essay on what they'd learned.

Her passion for reading over the years has amassed her with hours of pleasure. It wasn't until she stumbled upon fanfiction that her thirst to write overtook her world. She now resides in Central Florida with her husband and son, spending all her down time letting her creativity flow and characters grow.

Website: https://www.elenamreyes.com/

Find My Books Here:
https://www.bookbub.com/authors/elena-m-reyes

Email: Reyes139ff@gmail.com

facebook.com/ElenaMReyesAuthor
x.com/ElenaMReyes
instagram.com/elenar139
tiktok.com/@authorelenamreyes
bookbub.com/profile/elena-m-reyes

ALSO BY ELENA M. REYES

FATE'S BITE SERIES

LITTLE LIES

LITTLE MATE

HALF TRUTHS DUET

HALF TRUTHS: THEN

HALF TRUTHS: NOW

OMISSION

TERO (TBD)

MARCIA (TBD)

BEAUTIFUL SINNER SERIES

Each book is a standalone.

Now Live!

SIN (#1)

COVET (#2)

MINE (#3)

YOURS (#4)

RISQUE #5

OWN #6

Beautiful Sinner Spin-Off

CORRUPT

MY SINFUL VALENTINE

SAVAGE KISS

ONE RULE

(BOOK #2 LIONEL TBD)

(Marked Series)

Marking Her #1

Marking Him #2

Scars #2.5

Marked #3

(I Saw You)

I Saw You

I Love You #1.5

Teasing Hands Duet

Teasing Hands #1

Taunting Lips #2

SAFE ROMANCE:

Taste Of You

Doctor's Orders

Back To You

STANDALONES:

Craving Sugar

Stolen Kisses